Slices

of

Orange

A Collection of Orange County Fiction

Nancy Brooks Rayl

Editor

Nancy Brooks Rayl, Editor
Photograph, John C. Harrell
Cover Design, Nancy Brooks Rayl

Lightning Publications
532 South Raymond Avenue
Fullerton, California 92631
(714) 879-8300

Library of Congress Catalog Card Number: 94-72770

ISBN 0-9632702-9-x

Orange County

Short Story

Winners

Lou Ayala

Jim Coffin

Betty M. Farrell

Randy D. Freeman

Barbara Fryer

Sharon Gagon *Shara Gajn*

Mark Higgins

Marjory Hill *Marjory Hill*

Robert Livingston

Greta Macias *Greta Macias*

Rod Vickery

Esme Williams

Esme Williams

I would like to thank the following people for their unflagging support and help with this project from beginning to end: William Clarke, John Harrell, Betty Hillman, Lyn Kirk, and of course, the wonderful group at Lightning Publications, without whom you would not be reading these words.

Table of Contents

Lazarus

Robert Livingston
Laguna Hills

This is my first piece. Ever. The path that led me to writing has been like the road to Hana. I have staked claims and dug soil samples from British Columbia to the Yukon for a couple of years. I have tended bar at a yacht club in Newport Harbor. One summer I hauled cameras around on a Warhol film in Greenwich Village. I have cooked wild game for the 'rough and tumble' in Alaska. I did some hand glazing for a ceramic artist in Laguna. In my most recent, and most painful, endeavor I worked with a pack of terminally anxious accountants. They laid me off last year.

In Chinese writing the word "crisis" is formed by combining the symbols of two other words. Danger and opportunity. There is a profound symmetry in that.

I decided I'd take this latest "opportunity" to write. I knew instantly that this was for me. It's as if all my planets just lined up. The sword just slipped right out of the stone.

These days I'm working on my first novel. I do not write for fortune. My compass does not know that direction. And I have no appetite for fame. Fool's gold, that. Somebody who really wants it can have my fifteen minutes.

All I really want from my writing is the joy of doing it, nothing more. Well ... that and to sit in one night with the Rock Bottom Remainders. I hear they play the West Coast on occasion. I want them to know I'm here in (but not limited to) Orange County, and I am practicing every day. Although that doesn't seem to be a requirement.

Hey, it could happen. In the full measure of a lifetime the untapped, the untested and even the unsavory have a chance to leap off their cozy little front porch of mediocrity and run with the big dogs. In the years before his Sioux people called him Crazy Horse he was known across the badlands as "Curly".

Robert Livingston

1

Lazarus

A celebration of tropical fragrance rolled off the Pacific and over the bony finger of the Balboa Peninsula on the breath of an approaching storm. The delicate blend of floral, salt and citrus from the Baja pushed the perpetual brown haze north and replaced it with the sweet scent of renewal. Gun metal grey clouds marched over the southeastern horizon and expanded like smoke under a blue-black ceiling. The wind whistled while tall palms danced. A peak tide poured over the cement retaining wall that surrounds the Island in a rhythm so steady it was like watching the pulse of the sea. Freshly painted white private docks, that jutted out from the Island like the teeth of a comb, rode high in the choppy water. Instead of looking down onto the decks of the boats from the sidewalk you looked up at the gentle sweep of their white hulls. Out on the bay sailboats fought lonely battles as they wrestled against their lines. Rigging clanked a ragged staccato beat against hollow masts as they jerked back and forth like giant windshield wipers gone mad. Overhead a wedge of pelicans angled off the coast seeking shelter under the chalky cliffs of the upper bay.

The cottage homes along the south bay front looked like they had to fight for their spots, pulling their shoulders in, standing tall and jamming themselves into the front row. There was just enough room between houses for a person to walk through, no more. From his second story bedroom, Jeff glanced out the window at the flag on the Pavilion roof across the bay. It was starched northwest. He expected the worst and dressed for rain. Dawn was not going to break this morning, so he could not judge the time by the light. As a result, he checked his watch constantly like a man late for a train. Even small changes in the daily ritual unsettled Jeff. He did not want to be late again and lose his job.

Jeff was not fond of mornings. Living alone depressed him. He dressed and left the house quickly as if by leaving he could shake off the hollow feelings of his isolation. He tried marriage for a short time last year, but it didn't work out. It was over almost as soon as it started. The test drive was a little bumpy. After about six weeks, the new car smell was gone, and so was she. Fortunately the union produced no heirs.

He stopped the car short of the humpbacked bridge that led off the Island. A small gathering huddled under the blue and white striped awning at Dad's Donuts. the welcome aroma of roasted coffee seeped into the pre-dawn air. Cold hands wrapped around hot cups. People bowed their heads, prayer-like, pulling the rich steam up their noses. Looks like the usual assortment this morning, he thought, exercise freaks, dog walkers, old people who can't sleep, and night crawlers on their way home. Once in a while someone would show up who, it seemed to him, had no good reason at all for being there. Everyone was a little too verbose for Jeff. It was as if they were all members of some fraternity because they were drinking coffee together, outside in the dark. They conversed in that animated, over friendly manner, as if they were polar explorers who just happened upon each other in the wilderness. Jeff kept his eyes down. In this club, eye contact was an invitation for conversation. He had nothing to say. He was here for the coffee, thank you, which he drank in silence on the institutional green bus bench, room permitting.

Jeff Beardwood spends most days as a baggage handler for Air West. It is mindless work, and he's well suited for the job. He is diminutive but rugged with bushy dark hair that seems to grow wild everywhere except on the palms of his hands. Thick chest hair runs right up his throat and doesn't stop until just below the eyes, then picks up again at the forehead and continues around and down the neck, disappearing behind the frayed yellow collar of his uniform. Flax colored teeth are tiny, sharp and crowded. The impression is that his mouth contains slightly more than the recommended number. Short legs do not drop straight to the ground, but rather curl down cowboy style. The eyes are clear but they shift and also seem to be a little too close together. Sturdy forearms disappear into small calloused hands. He is strong for his size, having thrown around people's belongings for more than five years. On weekends he cuts up the Mojave Desert on a dirt bike. He is not one to waste his free time reading books.

Jeff started this day, like every day, at the Orange County Airport by sweeping up the claim tickets and cigarette butts around the three baggage carousels located halfway between the low slung main terminal and the two double wide trailers that serve as temporary terminals. Outside the smoked glass windows a row of commercial planes roosted passively on the tarmac. Workers swarmed over them like insects inspecting a dead bird. On the runway a small prop plane lifted off and disappeared into the overcast. Three more awaited clearance from the tower across the way. Soldiers on the front lines of commerce and industry off to skirmishes at first light.

A round metallic truck, as bright as a piece of polished Mexican silver, appeared and started to fuel the airliners. Crew members in orange jumpsuits shoved white umbilical cords, thick as pythons, up into the tail sections. Jeff could see the dreamy lines of the vapor dissolve into the thick morning air, like cream into black coffee. He doesn't avoid the fumes. He likes to be around them. After each deep breath he would drift into a world of nightmarish sounds and mirages.

Jeff stood inside the terminal looking through the glass door and smoking. Soon the people would start to filter in and breathe life into the steel and cement. He felt less important when they were there. They pushed right by him like he was invisible. Everybody in a hurry. Indifferent, disrespectful even. People with tickets to grand and exotic places. Places he could only imagine. Didn't they know that he was an important link in their travel chain? He controlled their property. He had power they knew nothing about. They could go anywhere, but their valuables would go where Jeff sent them. This internal conversation sent bitterness burning through Jeff's veins like a fast-acting poison.

Jeff operates the belt truck. It was more accurately a cart, but truck sounds better. It has only one seat for the driver. Just to his right, where the passenger seat would be is a long platform that stretches out twelve feet, like a diving board on a car. This platform is a heavy rubber conveyor belt. The driver can raise the front end up into the belly of the plane to carry the luggage up or down the ramp.

Flight 931 from San Francisco completed its long, lazy bank over the foothills and swung south on its final approach. Jeff pulled into slot 5A and waited for the plane. This was his favorite slot. It's situated well past the terminal, out of the boss' line of sight. With nobody watching he could be as rough with the luggage as needed. There had been a flood of complaints recently about damaged luggage. Jeff's boss had put the word out that effective immediately he was going to be monitoring everybody a bit closer. The boss said he would not tolerate any more mistreatment to luggage at 'his' airport. He assumed, incorrectly, that just showing them the whip would suffice. Jeff never saw the whip. He stopped listening after the bit about the monitoring. That was an unpleasant proposition. Jeff worked best when he worked unsupervised.

He resented his boss for having such an easy job and he wanted it as much as he ever wanted anything. This ambition evolved into spitting envy. At times he daydreamed himself sitting in the fat leather chair in the office behind the carousel, barking out orders with feet up. Nothing much to do but smoke cheap cigars and make sure others did the work. That was Jeff's compass heading. He saw nothing but that, and if some damage occurred along the way, so be it. Just the cost of doing business, he thought. He did not worry about the boss while he worked 5A.

4

The interiors of the planes were colder than usual today with the rainy weather along the seacoast. Jeff worked impatiently, flinging the bags to the lip of the cargo hold, then moving over and slapping them down on the belt. The more expensive the bag, the less respect he had for it. He liked to toss a nice Louis Vuitton a bit further than, say, an old duffel bag. The affluent travelers disturbed him the most. He liked to picture them at home opening their suitcase, picking at the broken pieces of some treasure. A momento from somewhere they may never return to. A sentimental souvenir. They would be brokenhearted. Maybe they would cry. Jeff delighted in serving his revenge cold.

At the bottom of the ramp a helper, in this case Tomas, pulled the bags off the belt and loaded them onto a white flatbed truck for the final leg of their journey to the terminal building. Something unusual caught Jeff's eye. In the far end of the compartment a small white animal carrying case with the word "Nugget" stenciled on the side in pink paint was secured to a ring on the wall by a leather strap. Jeff saved it for last. Just as he was dropping the cage onto the belt he turned his head for a split second to make sure the hold was empty. The next sound that reached Jeff's ears took his breath away.

Nugget had gone over the side. The cage never even established contact with the belt. Just plunged straight down, bounced twice, rolled on its roof and stopped. Tomas and Jeff stared at each other through the rain. Tomas seemed more amused than anything. Jeff turned his attention to the fallen cage, fish eyed and frozen. He held his breath and slid down the ramp on the seat of his pants. His stomach churned. Tiny beads of sweat pushed through the oily skin on his forehead.

No pet sounds came from the box. The sleeve of a vermilion sweater hung through the wire mesh of the door soaking up dirty rain water. Gingerly, he righted the cage and placed it on the transport truck. He looked around to make sure there were no other witnesses as he bent to look inside the box.

Before he could focus his eyes in the dark shadows of the cage he heard an engine hum in the distance, getting closer. He stiffened and cocked his head as it grew louder. His heart tried to punch its way out of his chest. Not the mammoth howl of a jet engine, but smaller, higher pitched. Jeff recognized the boss' truck. Without turning around, he pushed Nugget's box deeper into the compartment. Then he stretched, as if bored with the ease at which he performed his trade. He tossed a nonchalant glance at the truck as it passed him heading for the garage. Their eyes locked for a heartbeat. To Jeff, it seemed like minutes. He remembered to exhale.

Jeff listened for any hint of life from the white box. There was nothing but silence. He shut his eyes tight and listened harder. Nothing. When he knew the boss had rounded the corner he went back to the truck. He pulled the cage out to the tailgate and unlatched the square door. Nugget was on her back. Limbs bent at disturbing angles. Little pink mouth hanging open, tongue falling limp over her upper teeth. The eyes were only half open and showed no sign of pupils. Jeff knew the dog was dead.

The natural instinct of animals, when injured, is to lie on their stomachs to cover and protect their organs. When they're belly up, they're dead. He reached inside the door and slapped the dog's head. All that did was make Nugget's tongue flop over to the opposite side of her mouth. Nugget had left the building.

A darkness dropped on him like a guillotine. He stood alone in the rain, a picture of devastation. He could not swallow for the lump in his throat. Trouble seemed to find him like a twister finds a trailer park. He didn't know of any specific rules against killing a piece of Air West Baggage, but he was sure it would pull the brake on his managerial ascent. His self pity fit him like a glove.

Then the clouds seemed to part as a bolt of inspiration crashed down on Jeff. He wheeled on Tomas, who spoke very little English, put his finger to his lips and then pointed a stubby finger at him, pistol-like, moving his head left and right. Tomas understood 'no' in any language. Jeff punctuated the gesture, or threat, by raised eyebrows. 'Or else.'

Jeff took Nugget's box, coffin actually, and put it under the conveyor belt on his truck and drove to the terminal. He shoved the rest of the baggage from 931 through the rubber flaps that lead to the terminal carousel and broke for lunch. Jeff slowly re-read the clipboard for the instructions regarding the 'live baggage' on 931 while he clocked out. Nugget stayed in the truck, covered by a pair of bright yellow rain pants.

He parked his little truck in a corner of the yard down toward the south end of the runway where he knew it would stay undisturbed for a while, and headed for the employees parking lot. A squall moved through the area. The lazy drizzle shifted into a hard rain.

He put a match to a smoke as he turned the car south on MacArthur Boulevard. Russo's Pet Shop was just about three songs down the road leaving Jeff little time to strike a bargain with God. To this date there had been no vertical relationship but this situation screamed for desperate measures. If God would put a little white poodle in the pet shop for him he would pay Him back, in spades. He

6

committed himself to charitable deeds and Sunday worship for the duration of his unworthy little life. Another troubled soul who found the Almighty right there in the foxhole.

A six pack of kittens frolicked on the shredded paper floor in the window display. A pleading child tugged at her mother's coat, making all the usual promises that will be broken within an hour of the kitten's arrival at its new home. The left wall was all fish. A palette of dazzling colors darted around plastic rocks set in fine white sand. Artificial plants swayed to the waltz-like rhythm of the electric filters. Beyond the fish and just before the turtles and snakes, along the right wall, Jeff's salvation slept in a cage on the third tier.

Jeff, warm in the comfort of answered prayers, silently praised 'Him from whom all blessings flow'. The sudden reprieve watered his grateful eyes. That, and the pungent scent of puppy urine.

He dodged a hailstorm of pitches by an over zealous teen aged sales girl to purchase a wicker doggie bed, puppy food, rawhide to chew and toys that squeaked. These additional products, all part of a larger picture, didn't interest Jeff in the least. As long as a dog was alive at three o'clock, the pick-up time by a Mrs. Leonard Rimbau, Jeff would be happy. In fact, he was within spitting distance of happy right now. This dog was as close a match as he could possibly hope for. Maybe a little smaller than Nugget, but that might be explained by the rigors of modern travel. Also, the color was not quite right. The replacement was a shade or two lighter than the vanilla color of Nugget, but he figured with a little dirt he could darken her up.

This he did when he reached the employee parking lot. He settled Nugget's cold body in the center of the spare tire in his trunk and pulled a greasy rag over her limp little body like a shroud. This tenderness was genuine but too late for the dog.

Placing the cage on the shelf inside the baggage claim area was not an easy task. This needed to be a clandestine operation. Too much time had passed since Flight 931 touched down. He could always explain that he was just playing with the puppy on his lunch break, but if that deception could be avoided, so much the better. He cruised back and forth past the terminal, like a hungry lion prowling a water hole. It was after two when he saw his chance and slipped in unnoticed.

Once the dog was in place and he initialed the square on the clipboard, his muscles relaxed and his heart slowed. Hope softened his face. He stopped by Tomas' truck to go over his threats one more time. He really didn't worry too much about Tomas. Besides speaking little English, Tomas had that timid disposition Jeff noticed in a lot of Mexican workers around the airport. They consider themselves so blessed to be working in America, that they wouldn't say anything about anything. For little people like Jeff Beardwood this was a rare and pleasant opportunity to bully somebody.

Three o'clock arrived uneventfully. Jeff thought about getting some water for the dog, but decided that might bring unwanted attention. He had placed the cage near the top of the cabinet so it would be visible through the window from the tarmac. He worked the rest of the afternoon with one eye fixed on the window. By three-forty his features hardened again, his neck was stiff and his head throbbed with tension.

It was around four-twenty when he saw one of the porters reach for the cage and study the tag. Trying not to appear suspicious, Jeff slipped into the area behind carousel number one. A large woman wrapped in a silver fur coat leaned on the service desk waving a claim ticket. She appeared to be rather formally dressed for such an early hour. An electric blue hat attached itself to the side of her ice blue hair. It was donut shaped and flat as road kill. Evening jewelry clutched her throat. Stones as large as hummingbird eggs nested on plump fingers. Thick pasty foundation that old women, and undertakers, trowel on to camouflage the march of time, was applied generously. It was not working. It only seemed to highlight the wrinkles that ran deep like the heavy bark on a Georgia pine. A fat dash of crimson began on her cheek bones just under the eye and disappeared into nothingness over by her ears, like the tail of a comet.

By contrast, her companion was remarkable. A ripe red plum to the old prune. Early twenties, Jeff guessed. Maybe the daughter. She paced around like she had someplace to go. Jeff watched her move like a peasant eyeing a banquet. She had a Cadillac walk. Wide and luxurious. She placed one four inch stiletto directly in front of the other as if trying to walk an invisible thin line. The result was absolutely breathtaking. She walked like that even when she was standing still. A short black cotton skirt inched its way up bare milk-white thighs. It almost seemed to fondle her as she moved.

Jeff snapped back to reality on the heels of a short piercing screech. The older woman lifted her 'Nugget' out of the cage and was staring a hole right through the dog with eyes astounded. Thin raspberry red lips parted to reveal a small reserve of gold dental work. Her eyeballs rolled back in their sockets until just a new moon of an iris remained. She wobbled on swollen ankles, drunk-like, then fell straight back. The first thing to land (after 'Nugget') was her rump, followed immediately by the back of her head. Being a large woman, she fell long and she fell hard. The crack of solid contact between her old skull and the new cement resonated under the tin roof that covered the baggage claim area. Jeff shuddered. It took him back to the summer nights of his youth, when the spank of hickory meeting horsehide echoed over the outfield grass.

The 'plum' dove to help. The curious surrounded the fallen woman. Everything came to a complete stop except for the slow turn of the carousel pregnant with unclaimed baggage. A thin man felt for her pulse. Someone else screamed. The young woman cradled the old woman's head and wailed like a banshee. A thick fluid trickled out of the fallen woman's right ear, slowly at first, then in a steady stream. The cloudy red ooze painted the 'white zone'. The little dog caught the scent of fresh blood, stiffened her tail and buried her nose in it, breathing in crude short snorts.

The young woman dropped her head to the old woman's bosom. She mumbled her words inches from the old woman's heart. Jeff couldn't understand what was being said from his vantage point but the tone was clear. Desperate and pleading.

When there was no response she unleashed a spine-chilling, savage moan. It was a singular note soaked in agony. Otherworldly. As long as train smoke. It dwarfed the drone of the jet engines outside in the rain. Blood ran off the oily fox fur like rain off a rose petal.

An ambulance showed up eventually, but there was nothing to be done. Mrs. Leonard Rimbau expired right there on the ground by carousel number one. The green and black claim ticket still locked in the death grip of her left hand. The young men pulled her dress down before they hoisted her onto the gurney. They tried unsuccessfully to close her mouth before the sheet was pulled up.

The young woman, hugging her mother's hat close to her heaving chest, explained to a puzzled policeman. He looked up often, disbelieving, as he diligently took down every word. Nugget died in San Francisco three days ago while on vacation with the family. They left her with a local vet, who loaded the dog up with embalming fluid and sent her home in her little traveling box for a proper doggie funeral and interment in the Rimbau family crypt in the hills above Corona Del Mar.

Jeff lingered long enough to hear the explanation before he slipped outside into the rain. Lightning cracked over the foothills. Thunder as sharp as broken glass shook the air around him. He studied his watch. This day couldn't end fast enough for Jeff Beardwood. As he tried to get his mind around the events of the afternoon he wondered if his deal with God still counted. So much had changed since they last talked.

9

The Writing Class

Esme Williams
Laguna Niguel

My main character and I share a deep affection for a narrow coastal strip of Southern California which extends from Balboa to San Clemente. This section of land in Orange County is known as Zone 24 by Horticulturists and climatologists and is one of the few remaining Edens on our planet. Nature favors it, and the cultural and historical background enhances the ambience of stories, novels, poetry, plays and musical offerings created within its boundries.

Coastal features vary from the picturesque Balboa Peninsula to the boat colony at Newport Beach from which Santa Catalina and San Clemente islands can be seen on especially gifted days. The fascinating Back Bay area serves as a bird sanctuary and merges to the caves and tide pools of Corona del Mar. Dramatic cliff fingers extending into the ocean announce Laguna Beach. Farther south lie Dana Point Harbor and San Clemente beaches.

This entire area lends itself to horticultural experimentation and gardeners, both private and city, have beautified the land. The reds of coral and flowering eucalyptus contrast with the purples of jacaranda, agapantha and veronica. Variations in greens and texture of palms, ferns, and evergreens provide a lushness and serenity which challenges the frenzy of freeways. The smooth perfection of golf courses lie below foothills, green after rains, yellow with mustard, then toasted golden brown by summer sun.

The indigenous Indians enjoyed this paradise until interrupted by the Spanish who worked to create converts and missions. Years later American settlers arrived with claims of ownership. Following the Spanish-American War, Chinese laborers were brought in to help with railroad construction. In the years since, people from every state in the union and from many foreign lands have found this lovely area and added their varied cultures.

This is where I live and write.

Esme Williams

11

The Writing Class

Simon turned off Moulton Parkway into the Lake Hills Community Church complex and parked close to the writing classroom. He nodded to the half dozen people already seated and eased into the chair next to Angie. "Early this morning," he grinned. She smiled, enjoying his open, weatherbeaten face and lively eyes. "I woke at four, bush tailed, so made coffee and rewrote my piece. How did you do with the dialogue?"

"Bit stilted I'm afraid. Marianne said to try writing down conversations we hear -- doesn't seem to work for me." He glanced at the circle of chairs filling rapidly. "Good turnout."

The chatter among the group was growing more animated. "Who listens to Rush Limbaugh? -- I like Dennis Prager -- Dr. Viscott was my favorite."

"We have radio fans among us," Angie murmured.

"Good morning, People, good morning." The instructor walked in, brief case in one hand and microphone and loud speaker in the other. Marianne Blakely was over forty but as yet no grey showed in her long, shoulder length hair. She was the ideal instructor for this group: ages varied from fifty to early eighties and all were alert and enthusiastic. Some were bent on writing a life story for grandchildren, others passionately hoped to publish while a few, to their delight, were discovering a new mode of self expression. Marianne provided a low-key atmosphere -- more a meeting of like-minded adults than a typical college classroom. She encouraged, gently prodded, drilled techniques, suggested improvements and sat back and allowed creativity to kindle and flame. And what tales came from this circle of people! Several were foreign born and many had worked or fought overseas. Incidents of religious intolerance and racial discrimination were contrasted by wonderful remembrances of childhood days. All the joys and tragedies of the human condition were revived here. Humor played a great part in their writing as it holds hands with courage in positive survival.

Marianne handed out topic sheets for the month and briefly discussed the assignment for the following week. "Those engaged in long-term projects," she concluded, "may want to consider the assignment. If not, fine. For those still a little hesitant in topic choice, perhaps these suggestions will jog a memory or otherwise inspire. All I really ask is -- write."

The two hour class passed quickly as individuals read and absorbed a penetrating yet encouraging critique by companions and instructor.

Later, walking with Angie to their cars, Simon asked, "Will you join me for breakfast tomorrow, Angie? We could discuss next week's assignment."

"Why, thank you Simon. I'll call you tonight. OK?"

"Fair enough. Bye for now."

As Angie drove towards home she thought about Simon. This was the fourth semester they had taken Marianne's non-fiction writing class. Angie had enrolled in Saddleback Community College classes for some time, but Simon had moved to Dana Point just three years ago. She had liked him the moment she saw him and a casual, pleasant relationship had developed during their brief encounters at class. "A date!" she mused, not sure how she felt about it. The memory of lonely, difficult weeks and months following her husband's death returned with its accompanying sadness. Priorities had been shuffled and reshuffled over the years until a life plan emerged which satisfied. She believed the later years in life challenged one to reflection, and, as solitude was a requirement for reading and thinking, she minimized her social life. The writing class provided the shoulder-rubbing assurance of belonging to the human race. Her hobbies of writing, walking, gardening and needlepoint were an extension of the main focus of her life. The differing environments they provided renewed and comforted and often gave birth to new insights. Family visits were a rare pleasure as her three children lived in different states. "Don't cross bridges," she told herself and called Simon after dinner.

He was seated at a table on the sunny patio of the Fiesta Mexicana gazing at green hills cradling the small town. Angie greeted him. "What a wonderful morning!"

"Isn't it? I'm glad you suggested this spot."

"I've always loved San Juan Capistrano. Perhaps you'd like to wander through the Mission after breakfast?"

"Angie, let's do that some other time. I was wondering if you'd like to go whale-watching -- the season will be over soon. Is your day free?" he asked as she eased into her chair and gestured for coffee.

"I haven't finished my first draft" Angie answered slowly. "I like to write it Tuesday and let it sit for a few days before I tackle it again. Perhaps we could discuss plots. Our class is supposed to be non-fiction but Marianne is gradually encouraging us to branch out. A little combined inspiration might be helpful."

"We could do that on the water as well as here, do you agree?" She nodded and concentrated on the menu. "Mushroom omelette and English muffin -- toasted very brown, thanks." She smiled at the young waiter. After Simon ordered she questioned him. "Tell me, Simon, have you decided if you want to publish? The travel pieces you've read in class were fascinating."

"I think I'm too lazy. I don't mind writing occasionally -- I enjoy reliving the memories -- especially retrieving the details -- but I have absolutely no interest in meeting deadlines. They are the things I miss the least in my retirement. But I think you should try, Angie -- there's an element of truth about your pieces which has a great appeal."

He nodded to the young man with the coffee pot, "Thanks, and how much do you pay them for the privilege of working here, Carlos?" he teased. MY NAME IS CARLOS was printed on his lapel badge, and Carlos smiled, his white teeth and thick black hair shining in the morning sun. "It's a great spot on a day like this," he answered in his precise English -- the merest trace of accent proclaiming his Mexican ancestry. "But remember," he continued, "it can rain, burn you up, freeze, and the Santa Anas can blow. This morning -- we are all very lucky." He dashed off to other tables.

Simon turned to Angie. "Your piece outlining the trials of your great grandmother deserves to be published. It contains the elements of a family saga. Why don't you try?"

She thanked the waiter who served her food and began her breakfast. "I vacillate -- this omelette is very good by the way." She paused. "After I visit a bookstore and observe so much rubbish on the shelves, I think not. Other times I feel it would be very satisfying if I could publish something really worthwhile."

They ate in silence for a few minutes enjoying the sun and the cool, fresh breeze.

"Simon, I believe most people were drawn to our class seeking encouragement to write a life story for grandchildren. The changes in our lifetime have been mind shaking. You've never mentioned grandchildren."

"No, Dorothy and I had one child -- Stephen. He died when he was five -- heart -- he was always frail." He paused, and seemed to force himself to go on. "She didn't want to try again. It hit us both. We concentrated on careers, hobbies, travel. Our life was good. I miss her."

"How long has it been?"

"Almost four years. After six months I knew I had to get away from the house, Phoenix, our friends. I'd come to this area often on business and always enjoyed it. I sold everything except books, rented a place here for a few months, and then bought the town-house."

"And why the writing class?"

14

He smiled at her. "Let's leave the inquisition 'till later. Unless you want more coffee. It's almost time to leave for the harbor."

Maneuvering in traffic along Street of the Golden Lantern, Simon noted, "We've known each other for two years but actually know little about each other's lives -- yet I feel I really know you personally very well."

She agreed. "It's difficult to write and not reveal oneself."

"Yes, that's one reason I find it such hard work. I don't necessarily want to bare my soul to the world -- or even to the class. I keep hoping Marianne will come up with some formula for writing objectively yet effectively."

"She advises allowing the real you to be reflected."

He crossed Pacific Coast Highway as the light turned and stopped under the tall, graceful eucalyptus trees in the Harbor parking lot. "I've a couple of wind-breakers in the trunk -- there are some clouds moving in -- we might need them."

Later that evening Angie reviewed the day. It had been a long time since she had enjoyed male companionship. The day had been wonderful -- too misty to see the whales but Simon had proved to be an interesting and exciting companion.

As she drove along Golden Lantern the following Monday morning, Angie felt a stirring of exhilaration. Spring, she thought is such a beautiful season -- and my writing class -- always a pleasure. Grateful that the first surge of traffic had eased she enjoyed the patches of yellow and orange daisies along the roadside contrasting with the varied exotic colors of the bougainvilleas. Cross-streets allowed glimpses of hills, green and misty from recent rains. Before turning left on De Anza she gave a sentimental nod to the snow-capped Saddleback looming in the background. She passed the neat and colorful landscaping of the older homes along De Anza and drew a deep breath as the Laguna Heights foothills appeared -- green and tree studded, with homes clinging to hillsides reminiscent of European travelogues. A jog to Portola, a left on La Plata, and then she turned onto Crown Valley Parkway -- where the golden masses of acacia blossoms filled the air with perfume. Angie appreciated the many spectacular flowering trees and shrubs from Australia and Africa which grew happily in California. This state disappointed some people, she thought, because the seasons were mild and merged so gently. Those who loved the state noted the changes by the annual flaming of the coral trees, the gold of the acacias and by the particularly haunting purple-blue of the jacarandas. These colors

15

heralded warm, sunny days and an abandonment to sports and beaches.

As she left the April gold of Crown Valley and turned on La Paz she repeated the lilting street name softly to herself. "La Paz." Such an exotic mix of Spanish and Oriental cultures in one small community roused mingled emotions of strangeness and comfort. La Paz was an interesting street, she thought as she passed the lovely and spacious Regional Park, glanced at the man-made lake of recycled water so serene in the morning light and edged with trees, tables, chairs and barbecues. The stark, Babylonian-like structure of the Chet Holifield building squatted on the left. Angie laughed. "Only in California." She turned onto Moulton and on this last lap of the drive allowed herself to think about Simon. "I care for him," she acknowledged, "and I'm willing to get to know him better."

During the next two months, Angie and Simon spent at least two days a week exploring areas new to one or both. Simon enjoyed sailing with his friends but could not persuade Angie to join him.

"I love the beach," she told him, "but I find the ocean too intimidating in a small vessel."

He did persuade her to take day cruises to Catalina and Ensenada, and she enjoyed both. She planned trips to San Diego and escorted Simon through the Zoo, Sea World, and the Wild Animal Park. They spent a day wandering around the old World Fair buildings at Balboa Park and planned return trips. Several days they browsed through the tiny galleries in Laguna and lunched at the historic old hotel. As they enjoyed Clae's fine food and the lovely shoreline, Angie reminisced. "As a child I played in rock pools. I've always loved them."

Once they drove to Balboa pier and ate hamburgers at Ruby's, and Simon praised the surf which was smashing hard on the sand. "There's quite a rip-tide today."

Angie told him, "When the children were growing I drove to the beach five days a week every summer vacation -- it seems a lifetime ago. I sat on the sand and counted heads most of the time. I remember getting a ticket one day -- the streets to the beach had been changed to one-way and I hadn't noticed. Here I was driving headlong towards a policeman. I cried -- I guess my nerves were stretched at the time."

"I wonder why," Simon teased, "with only three kids." They laughed together.

One week Angie planned a morning at the "ziggurat" and as they neared the building Simon stared. "Shades of centuries past" he marvelled. "What a monstrosity! California is all color and light, opportunity and hope and here this sits -- emanating a brooding sense of

16

power and ruthlessness."

Angie burst into laughter. "Marianne would appreciate that rush from the heart." She parked and as they walked towards the building. She told him "Rockwell International built this in 1968 -- why the design I haven't discovered yet. It was never used -- aerospace cutbacks -- so the Government acquired it a few years later. Now it houses quite a variety of Government services -- National Archives files, genealogy records, I.R.S., Social Security, Immigration -- on and on -- it's a fascinating place. I thought I might write a piece on it for class sometime." They entered the Genealogy doorway and parted -- Angie to complete some research and Simon to wander and investigate.

Two hours later as they walked to the car Angie asked if he'd enjoyed himself. "Yes. This new technology they are introducing is a great help. It's called CD-ROM. I talked to the Project Leader and learned how to use it."

"Good." Angie nodded approval. "Next time we visit you can teach me. I'm looking for my great grandfather -- I think there's a story there."

Simon was interested. "That's an idea."

Later, as he slowed and stopped in front of Angie's small, two story house tucked away on a quiet street, he asked quizzically, "You still want to keep your weekends to yourself?"

"Simon, I'll see you in class Monday. I'm glad you enjoyed today. Goodbye."

As Simon drove home his thoughts were centered on Angie. He admired her neat appearance, pleasant manner, the varied aspects of her personality and her inner strength. She's a comforting person to be around, he thought, but she doesn't really need me in her life. Perhaps I should leave her alone. He felt vaguely dissatisfied, and reaching home, poured himself a drink and walked onto the balcony. He watched the young people splashing in the pool below. "Everyone needs companionship," he finally decided. "I'll ask her next week." He walked inside and settled down to his current reading.

At the next class Marianne glanced at the sign-in sheet. "Simon, what do you have for us today?" Simon's writing to date had consisted of various accounts of travel. They were objective, light, and fascinating.

"I'm trying dialogue in a piece I've called "The Proposal." He reached for the microphone, adjusted it and began to read. This piece was from the heart -- a lonely man's request for a woman to share his life. As he read, the class listened -- touched, and wondered if his friendship with Angie had deepened, or if he had found someone else.

Marianne was generous with her praise. "So moving, Simon. The dialogue directs very well. Comments, class?"

There were the usual comments and helpful criticisms. Angie was still, wondering if this was a proposal or if she had lost a good friend.

As they walked towards their cars Simon asked "Well, Angie, will you?"

In spite of tumultuous thoughts, she laughed. "Simon, what a romantic you are!"

"Well?"

"Let's drive to my place. We'll have lunch on the patio and talk about it."

They decided to marry the third week of summer break. Two weeks remained of the spring semester and Angie and Simon made their plans. A simple wedding with witnesses only and a reception on Angie's patio pleased them both. Her garden was always beautiful but extra color was planted for the event. She hoped the children could come, and she wanted her few long-time friends with her for the celebration. Simon wrote to his nephew in Phoenix and asked two of his sailing friends to attend. The weeks passed quickly. She was half dozing one night when the phone rang. "Hello" she murmured sleepily.

"Mrs. Morse, this if Jeff Pritchard, a friend of Simon."

"Is anything wrong?"

"I'm sorry. He's been taken to Mission Hospital. We were playing cards -- a stroke, I think."

"Oh, no."

"I'm leaving for the hospital now. Would you like me to pick you up?"

"Thank you." Angie gave him directions to her home and dressed quickly with shaking hands. "Simon," she said, "Simon, please."

"Coffee?" Jeff handed her a foam cup. They were alone in the hospital waiting room and the clock showed 2:30 a.m.

"Thank you, Jeff, you're a good friend."

"I doubt they'll let us visit him tonight" he said. "Let's see what the doctor says, and I'll take you home."

Angie showered and dressed after Jeff left. The doctor's guarded, "We'll know more tomorrow" had given little comfort. She went about her accustomed routine deliberately knowing it was the best way to cope.

At the hospital a few hours later she caught the doctor after his rounds. "It's severe" he said. "A partial recovery would be long and difficult, but, if all goes well, it's possible."

Angie returned to the hospital in the afternoon and sat beside

Simon's bed for a few moments. He was pale and remote and did not recognize her. She squeezed his hand. "I'll come again tomorrow when you're feeling better, Simon" she said softly.

She visited him morning and afternoon for the next week. She talked quietly to him of the plans they had made and often she repeated the life experiences told by the members of their writing class, hoping that somewhere inside he was conscious of her voice and her love and need of him.

Simon died two days before their planned wedding day.

As she drove along Golden Lantern the following September, Angie remembered her joyous spring drive months before. The season was old now -- hills were brown and the trees dusty. The only flowers blooming were the tried and true nursery specials set out by the City. A few leaves were beginning to wither -- winter would be early this year. It was only nine o'clock but the heat was unbearable. She turned on the air conditioner. Dog days! The park and lake were deserted -- the children had returned to school. As she passed the ziggurat she recalled Simon's first reaction to it, and tears filled her eyes.

She turned onto Moulton, concentrated on traffic, and drove the last few miles to the writing class.

Worms

Mark Higgins
Irvine

Why do I write?

I. CHARACTER

I could make myself sound intelligent by rewording Jung's transcendent function of literature. I could mention Joseph Campbell's beliefs of the shaman-like duties of the writer in this, the century of alienation. I could talk about myth, archetypes, imagination, the objective correlative. I could even throw in a quote or two from the Bible.

II. CONFLICT AND SYMBOLISM

Instead, let me talk of guilt. Of fear. Of this damned computer (antagonist) that my father (mythological archetype) bought for me 15 years ago (troubled past) when I dropped out (failure) of law school (establishment) and told him I wanted to be a writer (hero).

III. CHARACTER MOTIVATION

Pretty cool of my father, to buy me a computer--booting me up rather than booting me down. Instead of implying "you owe me something," with his gift, he seemed to be saying "you owe you something."

IV. CHARACTER INSIGHT

That something is the only thing that seems to last, at least for me. That something is story.

V. FLASHBACK LEADING TO THEMATIC EPIPHANY/RESOLUTION

My father and his seven brothers told stories, comedic, thrilling, climactic. They inherited storytelling from their mother, my grandmother, who still, at 87, can spin a yarn better than anyone I know. Story, for my family, was and is synonymous with intimacy. Huddled around the kitchen table, we share our experiences, the myths of our lives, and these are the things, more than name, more than blood, that bind us.

Mark Higgins

Worms

Ziggy Beckman times it well; when he hears the excited, shrieking voices of Phuoc Nguyen, his daughter Thao, and the three grandchildren returning from a day of fishing at the Newport Pier, he exits his apartment quickly, races to the front of the Ridgemont Apartments, and poses, hose in hand, waiting. As the children's sneakers pad the cement walk, as their giggles echo through the courtyard, Ziggy's blood rushes, like the water through the rubber hose. The door clicks open and the Nguyen clan shoots out like a burst from the nozzle, a colorful spray of rainbow, cool and refreshing.

Phuoc holds the fish up for Ziggy to see. "Worms good!"

Ziggy shudders. Worms, he knows, are bad.

"You no like fishing?" Phuoc asks.

Hate fishing. Ziggy can't touch worms. When he is turning the soil out front amid the rhododendrons, sometimes Ziggy fears the worms, feels he might meld into the sod, that the worms will find him, burrow into his soft and rotting flesh.. Sometimes he dreams the worms will escape from Phuoc's plastic bucket, climb the walls and sneak up on him while he is sleeping.

Later that evening, Nguyen's daughter, Thao, is busy corralling the three children, leading them to the station wagon parked by the curb. Ziggy pulls the hose and pretends to concentrate on his plants; Nguyen shuffles to the car in his slippers.

Ziggy peeks over his shoulder as Phuoc bends his body and climbs into the rear seat, all three grandchildren smothering him with dirty kisses and sticky hands as they head out for ice cream. Phuoc turns and catches Ziggy's eye before Thao shuts the door. Thao walks around to the driver's side, hops in, and pulls away.

Against the wishes of Phuoc's daughter Thao, Ziggy supplies Phuoc with Lucky Strikes. Phuoc joins him at the north corner of the parking lot Monday through Friday at noon. There, like two teenagers, they sneak puffs of the illicit weed into their lungs, a cancerous co-conspiracy. A butt dangles from Phuoc's mouth as he holds his fishing rod in hand and casts the line across the carport driveway. The weighted end sails to the far side of the lot. Phuoc offers Ziggy the pole.

Ziggy says, "I'm no fisherman."

Ziggy Beckman is alone in this world. So embarrassed is he of his condition that he begins to tell Phuoc Nguyen fish stories about his big family in Connecticut, his seventeen grandchildren, his upcoming remarriage to his second wife, a woman named Edna Hillary.

Edna was a plain woman, for the most part. If you seen her sittin' on a bus you wouldn't think nothin' of it. Except once she stood up you'd notice that stuck to her side, from her armpit to just below her ribs, was a thick piece of flesh that joined her to her Siamese twin sister, Millie.

Ziggy does have a picture of himself with a set of Siamese twins, an old daguerreotype of him standing behind the two girls, his arms around their shoulders.

"This here's Edna on the left," Ziggy says to Phuoc. "We fell in love soon as we laid hands--I mean eyes--on each other."

Phuoc understands some, but not all. He continues to cast his line out, across the carport.

Ziggy grows to hate the Sunday fishing trips that Phuoc Nguyen takes with his family to the pier. He listens anxiously for their return, mid-afternoon. Finally he hears the giggling grandchildren, the slam of the security gate, the soft voice of Thao, and finally, the shuffling slippers of Phuoc Nguyen. Ziggy listens to them below him, the banging of cupboards, the preparing of the meal, the smell of fish rising in through his windows. By seven p.m., when they begin to leave, Ziggy rushes out front. He is on his knees in the shrubbery. He does not turn around. He knows too well what happens behind his back. He visualizes it all, the daughter holding the door open, the little ones piling into the back seat, Phuoc Nguyen tumbling into their arms, the slam of one door, then another. The engine turns over, rumbles, the car pulls away. Ziggy sometimes dreams of turning into a fish, flopping before the Nguyens, his eyes mournful, enticing them with his imminent death. Though fearful of worms, Ziggy would consider swallowing one if there was some guarantee that he would be caught.

The softness of the dirt in his palms repulses him. He stares at his hand but can't differentiate between his skin and the earth. He feels a wriggle. He jumps up and rushes to the spigot, cranks the valve, and washes himself alive.

Another Sunday, after fishing. The weather is warm, the sky clear blue. While Thao is cleaning and cooking the fish, Phuoc takes his grandchildren into the pool. "Papa! Papa!" they scream as Phuoc enters the water waist deep, his long pants rolled up past the knee for no apparent reason as he is soaked to the belly button. The kids scream and splash at their grandfather as Ziggy watches from his window.

"Stay away from the deep end!" Ziggy yells, limping down the stairs and toward the pool. The younger twin, Jon-Jon, splashes Ziggy and laughs. "Hey!" Ziggy points his cane down at the kid playfully. Jon-Jon grabs it, laughing in high-pitched shrieks as Ziggy swirls him through the water.

From the shallow end corner of the pool Phuoc Nguyen laughs, as does Thao, who peeks out from the kitchen window.

"Do it to me!" squeals the eldest, a four year old named Jenny.

Jim-Jim, the other twin, reaches out from the deep end to save a drowning Japanese beetle as Ziggy gives Jenny a ride.

A scream. Thao is bounding out of the apartment, toward the water. Jim-Jim, in his efforts to save the droning beetle, has tumbled into the deep end and sinks. Phuoc goes down after him and stays down. Thao clutches her heart at the edge of the pool. Ziggy is in the water before he has time to think. There is a second or two of silence, just the swirl of the surface of the water after Ziggy's plunge.

Was a circus in town. She was in the sideshow. All we needed was one date, and we knew right there we were in love. Wasn't nobody around wanted to marry us, though. Talk of polygamy and against God's law and freaks of nature. Fools. We were in love. I wanted to marry Edna, only Edna. Wanted to make love to Edna, only Edna.

It was strange, with Millie getting dragged along everywhere, but after a while I didn't even notice. When we'd say, 'Millie, we want to be alone,' she'd oblige us and occupy herself with some needlepoint.

Finally did find a minister to marry us. Claimed he was a minister, anyway. Cost us $200, but worth every penny.

Three heads erupt through the surface, mouths gasping, coughing. Thao races to the side and clamps her child, then her father, as Ziggy clenches the backs of their shirts. Jim-Jim shrieks madly and spits up chlorinated water, clinging to his mother tenaciously. Throughout all of it, the other two children watch from the steps of the shallow end, holding onto Ziggy's cane as if it is a float.

"Bad bug!" yells Jim-Jim, crushing his cowboy boots down upon the back of the beetle. The shell pops and crunches.

Thao thanks Ziggy profusely. "You save my family." She hugs him.

Sunday. Ziggy breaks up the clods of dirt around his rhododendrons that line the front lawn of the apartment. The plants have started to bloom white petals. He hears a car pull up along the curb behind him.

He hears a cough. He turns around. A huge station wagon waits by the curb. Thao, the kids, Phuoc wave to him. Phuoc gets out, shuffles up to Ziggy Beckman.

"I have something to tell you," Ziggy says. "It's about the Siamese Twins."

Phuoc Nguyen nods.

"I lied."

Phuoc shrugs. He has heard his share of fish stories.

"Remember when I told you I only made love to Edna? Well, it was awfully dark in that bedroom of ours, and I gotta admit, one time we made love--the best love we ever made--and I thought everything was fine but next mornin' got up at the table and kissed Edna and called her my midnight lovebird but she shrugs me off and says she slept like a log since early evenin' and there's old Millie sittin' there with a smile on her face as wide as my first wife's bottom."

Phuoc is smiling as he turns around to leave.

"Wait, there's more," says Ziggy.

"No more story."

"You gotta hear the end of this. Edna and Millie, they got separated. Then me and Edna, we got separated. I come to find, me and Millie were the ones in love all along!"

He ignores Ziggy and whispers to him. "You got Luck Strikes?"

Ziggy nods.

"I got good worms. I put on hook for you, huh?"

Ziggy squints his eyes, leans forward in confusion.

Phuoc opens his car door, motions for Ziggy to get in. Ziggy does. As they sit in the back seat, the children wriggling around them, Phuoc places a fishing pole in Ziggy's hands, then says to him, "Thao want you keep. She say you better fisher than me."

Ziggy grips the pole, then looks down, sees the plastic container filled with worms at his feet. He softly pushes them to the side. Kicking over with a rumble, the car pulls away. The sun shimmers upon the road, making it glimmer like a rushing river; the car a huge fish swimming upstream.

Cafe Talk

Rod Vickery
Mission Viejo

Orange County politics may be a throwback to some Neanderthal age of commies under every table, but the county's natural beauty and growing cultural mix create an ideal environment for writers and artists. I write poetry and short fiction because I think less is more and few of us can maintain attention spans beyond exaggerated sound bites. Yet against all odds I continue to belt out a novel, "The Feiffer and Frome Fat Farm", set in Orange County. Many Orange County celebrities appear in the novel including one hack congressman. "Cafe Talk", my short story selected for this anthology, may end up as a chapter for the novel. Between bouts of writing I run trails throughout the Santa Ana mountain range, and to keep broccoli on the table I operate a sports related business in Mission Viejo.

Rod Vickery

Cafe Talk

We are sitting in TiaJuana Style, a Mexican restaurant with high beams and ceiling fans that rotate too slowly to disperse a mad mix of cilantro and the cheap cologne of Mexican waiters. Mariachi music drifts in the dining room from the bar. Everyone at our table, including the amateur stripper from Captain Creams, is drinking. The hair stylist from Laguna Beach is on the edge of drunk. He waves at me from across the table with two gold ringed fingers that lift off his glass each time he brings it to his lips to drink. I appear to be the only one concerned about his deteriorating condition. Others at the table, an assortment of vague business acquaintances involved in an unnecessary development project, are happy and tap their feet against chairs to the beat of the mariachi band.

The blond woman with the custom nose and eyes too far apart for dancing turns to me and smiles with bonded teeth. Her teeth are bright as a Crest ad, and I imagine her mouth making love to me under the table. She is almost pretty but too much rouge and lipstick have taken the edge off her natural good looks. She looks familiar and I am sure we have met before.

"And how is Rebecca?" she asks a little too loudly.

The conversation stops as if on cue. Rebecca is my estranged wife. She is planning to marry the Mercedes mechanic who serviced my foreign cars for years. I had never thought of Militas Peak as anyone other than a nice looking car mechanic, certainly not my wife's lover. I always thought his fees were exorbitant.

"I don't know. I haven't seen Rebecca in six months." I lie, but my tone is sufficiently nonchalant to ward off suspicions of hurt. No one looks askance. The young hair stylist is intrigued and waves again clutching a Long Island Ice Tea. The blond woman with eyes too far apart comes at me like a shot.

"I saw Rebecca three or four months ago at South Coast Plaza. She looked wonderful. New hairdo."

"She was always changing hairdos. I'm glad she looked good." I pause then add, "How good did she look?"

TiaJuana Style is filling with patrons from the local churches for a last brunch. The children look uncomfortable in dresses and tight suits and scrunch up their faces as they pass our table. We don't look like churchgoers. The parents smile at us disapprovingly. The banker from New York is getting loaded, his voice an octave too high for the churchgoers.

28

"Well, Jeffrey, if you must know," the blond begins again in a wispy, confidential tone that hovers over the table like a persistent fly. "Rebecca had a marvelous boob job. And she must be working out twenty-four hours a day because her calves look like coiled springs. I'd say Rebecca is close to a nine, not bad for forty."

"Forty-one," I remind everyone at the table.

As we prepare to leave the restaurant, Tony Latimer magnanimously picks up the tab, and lets everyone know from where generosity comes by splashing his platinum American Express card on the table like a spilled drink. Outside the sun is shining and the Santa Ana mountains glow under faint puffs of cloud. There is a chill in the air. The late morning autumn weather reminds me again why I live in Southern California. Goodbyes are exchanged and the blond with the sharp nose approaches.

"I hope I didn't say anything about Rebecca that upset you." Her voice is soft, almost a whisper with a hint of intrigue.

"Not at all," I lie again. "I hope Rebecca is happy now." The words are barely out of my mouth and I want them back. They float in the air between us like a flock of gulls.

"You know, Jeffrey, I like Rebecca a lot." The blond hesitates, then looks directly into my eyes. "I just never thought you two were good for each other."

"Oh?"

The others wave again as they start across the newly asphalted parking lot bedecked with orange cones looking like an unplanned obstacle course. Two valets in ridiculous tuxedos display their annoyance at our earlier refusal to use their services by turning their backs on us and engaging in exaggerated conversation. The hair stylist and the generous banker from New York climb in a new BMW 735 together.

"Yes," the blond continues in a reverential tone. "The few times we met, you impressed me as someone who required more...more stimulation."

I feel the climbing sun in my eyes and regret I left my Ray Bans at home. I am squinting at the blond woman like a test pilot standing in front of a ferocious wind tunnel.

"I'm sorry. Your name was....," my voice trails off as I fumble for an approach.

"Judith. Judith Avenue. I worked with Rebecca at Nordstroms."

"Of course. How careless of me." I breathe again. "Would you like to join me this afternoon for a neighborhood barbecue?"

"I'd be delighted. But I'm surprised."

"Surprised? That I'd be so bold to ask out one of Rebecca's friends?"

"Oh no," she dismisses the suggestion. "Surprised you eat meat."

We both laugh. "Judith, honestly, we can barbecue broccoli and cauliflower all afternoon." Judith laughs again and her mouth opens wide like an invitation. The excess rouge and lipstick have become assets. Strange how perceptions change as morning light lingers into afternoon. We laugh again and stroll as old friends across the parking lot to my chariot gleaming like ripe fruit in the California sun.

The Cove

Marjory Hill
Laguna Beach

A few years ago Robert Nathan was asked on a TV show what he was doing. He replied that he was writing his autobiography, and he thought everyone who could, should. I already had a drawer filled with one unpublished novel and several short stories. Why not an autobiography to fill another drawer? I wrote my life. Since then I have updated it with journals. I enjoy writing. It reinforces the pleasurable and is therapy for the troublesome.

I was born in Los Angeles in 1913, and while I did not live in Orange County until I was fifty-seven, many of my happiest memories are centered in the beaches of the Orange Coast. When I was in high school and college, Balboa was the place to go. It was a teenager's paradise. We aquaplaned in the harbor, taxied out to the recently constructed jetty and raced into the roller coaster waters of the open sea. What a thrill! We explored the coves of Laguna, and I was hooked for life.

In the forties my sister had a pre-fab beach cottage in Beacon Bay on the Mainland facing the back side of the island. That is where my children learned to swim. Before long they were swimming across the channel to the island. Their cousins, five years older, took them out in their rowboat, and a few years later my son sailed around the island in his cousins' Snow Bird. I never worried. The world was safe back then.

Since 1970 I have lived on a hill in Laguna with a sweeping white water view a half mile above the cove. There have been changes; there has been growth. But nothing that has happened has diminished my love for my own "Slice of Orange."

Marjory Hill

The Cove

It was love at first sight the day I discovered the cove. We had recently returned to Southern California from the Midwest where my husband's business had taken us. I had tried out several other coves-- this one was too crowded, that one was thick with seaweed, another one was noisy when, like Goldilocks, I happened upon the one that was just right. Lots of sand castle engineers under the watchful eyes of young mothers, and a cluster of grandmothers interspersed with a smattering of grandfathers playing card games until the ladies pulled on white bathing caps--the old fashioned kind it's so difficult to find, the ones with chin straps--and eight strong they gamboled down to the surf, dove through the breakers and swam out to the point.

They fascinated me. I was in my late fifties at the time. They looked to be considerably older. Even though I had spent a goodly portion of my summers on the beaches of Santa Monica and Hermosa in my childhood and youth, I was timid. The very notion of diving through a breaker brought ice water to my veins. Yet here were these ladies, surely my seniors, prancing down to the water and diving in. If they could do it, so could I. And I did.

I noticed that most of them were wearing two piece bathing suits. Reluctantly I had foresworn the luxury of a warm sun on a bare midriff some ten years earlier in favor of decorum. Yet these ladies, whose bodies were no trimmer than mine, showed no signs of selfconsciousness. If they could do it, why not I? I still wear two piece suits in this day of near nakedness even though I must have them made to order to cover my aging girth.

When the tourists left and the seagulls returned, very few swimmers remained. My ladies, as I grew to think of them, swam in their group. I swam solo. And so it went into the second autumn. By November, they and I were about the only diehards in the water. Still they swam in their group, and I swam solo. Until the day Jean approached me, asking me to be their surrogate leader. Their leader, the lady in front of whose home they congregated, was on vacation. That was my entree to the cove's inner sanctum.

These were no ordinary women. Their group included four retired teachers, a former musical comedy star, a violinist. They were educated, well travelled, cultivated, mentally and physically active. The senior member of their group, Sharon, was a retired kindergarten teacher, and I'll bet she manned a tight ship. She was tough, crafty, needlessly penurious. (On her travels she ate her evening meal in her room enjoying the leftovers from the breakfast table.) It was said she was a mad woman at the wheel of a car. Fortunately, I managed to avoid putting that assessment to a test. She had a saying that summed her up--"Not to worry." She used it whenever she got a speeding ticket. She used it whenever she was tumbled in the breakers. And following her mastectomy she used it when her falsie floated out to sea. Imperturbable. When her daughter was murdered by a deranged house painter, it was Sharon, by then in her eighties, who held the family together. A few days before her death at eighty-nine, she attended a luncheon. She looked beautiful. No longer able to hold any food on her stomach, she toyed with it so skillfully that I, sitting next to her, was unaware that she could not eat. From the luncheon she went home, removed her mask of make up, took to her bed and died.

Next in seniority is dear, charming Joy, who, at ninety-six, is still alert and culturally active. I cannot keep up with the swelling number of her great grandchildren and great great grandchildren. She spawned a prolific clan.

Joy arrived in New York from London with an Irving Berlin show when she was a girl of eighteen. She married the leading man at nineteen, and had the first of their three children at twenty. She lives by herself in a dear little cottage that she rents from her daughter--she will have it no other way--often getting around by foot or bus even though her solicitous daughter lives just blocks away.

Margaret is ninety-four. Until a month or so ago she was playing tennis. Then some old back injuries felled her, forcing her to give up her aerobics class as well as her tennis, and introducing her to the anti-inflamatory drugs that keep most of us going. Her cancer of the throat creeps along slowly, and we fully expect her and Joy to ring in the twenty-first century.

In her day Margaret was a dynamo, back-packing in the Sierras, the Alps, and the Andes, bike riding to the University of Irvine campus from her Laguna home along busy Pacific Coast Highway. Her most recent trip was to the Galapagos Islands, which she found to be strenuous but informative.

Our host and hostess on the beach were Harry and Doris. In summer Harry was the village pharmacist. Winters he taught chemistry at a prestigious boys' school. He was a cantankerous old bastard, tough and penurious. Doris was a sweet, gentle peacemaker. Together they were the self-appointed keepers of the cove, raking it, sweeping the several dozen steps that lead to it, and since there is no access to it for mechanized equipment, they cleaned it up after the occasional heavy storms when the turbulent surf disgorged broken boats and tree trunks, chopping the wood and lugging it up the cliff to their home for firewood.

Harry and Doris built their first home on a side street not two blocks from the waterfront. Later they bought a second home just steps away from the stairs to the beach. When they were offered the opportunity to buy a parcel of land on the waterfront for thirty thousand dollars, Doris said, "We can't afford to buy it."

Harry said, "We can't afford NOT to buy it." The house they built wasn't much as waterfront houses go, but taken together the three houses represented a net worth of between two and three million dollars. Yet they walked to town, lugging their supplies home on foot to save wear and tear on their ten year old car. They grew their own vegetables, and in the twenty years of our acquaintance I never knew Doris to have a new dress.

Harry was a public figure, active in the affairs of the city, mayor for a time, an art judge on the Festival board. (What his qualifications were for that, I can't imagine.) But his primary occupation was arbiter of the morals on the cove and custodian of its marine life. Every morning he and Doris raked the beach and readied it for his guests--lucky were we, the chosen few. He sat in his chair facing the sea, enforcing the laws of his cove. Woe to him who dared to trespass. Harry would approach the intruded, explaining that he paid taxes to the mean high tide line, and the beach to that point was his living room, reserved for his guests. Wherever his ever-watchful eyes spotted a bucket, he checked it out for contraband sea life. Wherever a beer can was raised, he cited the City Ordinance prohibiting alcohol on the beach. Hanky panky, no matter how innocent, while not exactly against the law, was not up to Harry's interpretation of proper cove decorum. Boomboxes were out. (And I was grateful.) Picnics were discouraged. (They drew ants.) Divers were driven off. (Their gear cluttered.)

Usually he intimidated offenders into submission. Not so one time when a stunning, sophisticated couple spread their blanket not six feet from Harry's living room, opened their picnic hamper, turned on their radio, took out champagne glasses and poured the bubbly. Instantly Harry was on them, explaining about the living room and the waterfront taxes, citing the law against alcohol and the potential for ants. The gentleman (for he surely was one) thanked Harry courteously for the information as he poured another round of the bubbly. We guests held our breaths. Three times Harry approached the poachers; three times the gentleman thanked him and poured more bubbly. That was the only occasion on which we witnessed his defeat.

Only once did we see Harry compromise his standards. One day a graceful young thing, wearing a topless sarong, sat herself crosslegged on the beach. Our men, the card players, sat transfixed, holding their breaths waiting for Harry to lower the boom. But to our amazement he never moved a muscle. Later Doris asked him why he had let the infraction pass. He replied, "She wasn't drinking, she wasn't noisy, and she did enhance the view."

Jean was our ingenue with the pursed lips and the raised pinkie. Regretfully her beaded sweats and ankle strap sandals didn't jibe with the battle-ax face and lumpish body God had seen fit to mete out to her. She pouted and sulked, and sometimes we wished she were not a fixture on the beach, but she was. Her father had owned one of the few village stores in the early days, and she had been swimming in the cove for sixty years--as long as anyone in the group. Jean's second husband, a somewhat doddering gentleman, played a dashing Lochinvar to her Lady Ellen, rushing down to the water's edge whenever she emerged from her swim to wrap her in an oversized beach towel and escort her back to her chair while the other ladies returned to under their own steam.

The cove was not new to my ladies. They came when they were young. Their children grew up making sand castles on the beach, as their grandchildren did, and their great grandchildren do to this day.

In summer the younger women who lived around the cove joined the group, and one by one, as they retired, their husbands became regulars. They brought imagination, ingenuity, and vitality to the life of the cove. Their gin rummy game evolved to a year-round tournament. They organized the golf and bought the kayaks that looked so intriguing, streaking across the water and around the bend, that I badgered my husband to take me out. Our timing was not the best. We met a wave head on, plowing straight through it instead of over it. A swimmer rescued my hat while we bailed water to stay afloat. Our return trip was no less dramatic. We almost made it to shore when a wave capsized our boat giving us a sand bath. After that we left the kayaks to the younger generation where they belong.

The men planned the social events: Fourth of July--hot dogs and kids. Beach parties--suckling pigs, prime ribs, or legs of lamb spit roasted with potatoes and corn, pit roasted. The cove was ours. Paradise.

Nothing lasts forever. When Harry and Doris died, Doris first, sitting on her bench and gazing out across the ocean she loved, and Harry a few months later, their living room was invaded. The divers moved in spreading their gear from one side to the other. The boomboxes blared, and one by one we lost my ladies--all except Joy and Margaret, but they can no longer struggle down those dozens of steps. No one swims now but Joy's son-in-law, my husband and me. The younger women are sun-shy, and the cove now belongs to a new generation.

There are times, though, when my ladies are there. I know they are. I can hear them, and I can almost see them. Like the time when we had hurricane waters that brought towering surf to churn and broil through patches of cobalt blue. The darkened waters were teeming with anchovies and sardines that lured the neighborhood gulls, flocks of visiting pelicans, and a gathering of foreigners--diminutive terns that glistened in the stormy sky. On the shore, what was left of it as the angry surf swept stray beach towels, slippers and a deck of the gin rummy players' cards out to sea, we watched the spectacle. To my right, a hundred or more pelicans took over, diving and chattering as they pushed and shoved the resident seagulls aside. They did not intimidate the little terns. Snow white, slender, wide of wing, these delicate little birds glided above the fray, fearlessly diving straight as a plane shot out of the sky, fifty feet or more into the inky pools of anchovies. To the left of me, the ocean was splashed with green from the seaweed that twisted and frothed in the volatile currents. I sensed that my ladies were there, marveling at such beauty.

The next day the surf dropped, but the anchovies and pelicans remained. The water was dark and murky. Should I swim? "Of course," I heard my ladies whisper. I felt as I swam along that I might be in the River Styx. Beneath me an opaque, gray blanket of anchovies undulated. The swarm of pelicans moved aside to make a narrow path for my passage, but as I swam between two columns of those long-beaked monsters, it occurred to me that they just might mistake me for a large juicy fish! "Nonsense", said my ladies. Why, I wondered, was I out here? Because it was beautiful. Because it was beautiful. Because they would be out here if they were here. "Not to worry," said a familiar voice from out of the past. "Take your swim." And I did.

The Perfect Escape

Sharon Gagon
Garden Grove

I was born and raised in Southern California. I have called Orange County my home for fourteen years. Considering my background, it seems only natural that the beach would provide the backdrop for this short story.

I have always found the written word to be a great creative and emotional outlet. It was a fourth grade early morning writing class which first opened up this new avenue of expression. The fact that I was willing to give up an hour of sleep, going completely against my character, immediately impressed my parents and proved my dedication. I have been writing ever since, working around three very welcomed interruptions by the names of Nicole, Christopher and Michael. They are my contributions to the talented pool of Orange County writers. Each child has, in some state of completion, a short story, novel, or poem. Each one with their own computer files of "works in progress."

When I'm not writing, playing mom, or raiding a See's Candy store, I enjoy physical activity. I love to play tennis, ride my bike, and hike in Yosemite. My personal challenge next year is to climb Half Dome. I like to read the classics, writing which has withstood the test of time. I love to read Shakespeare and am constantly in awe, always amazed at his "timely" insights.

I love to travel, to see places I've only heard of or seen through someone else's words. Each new place and every new experience is writing material. A personal high was a trip to Stratford-upon-Avon, complete with a performance of Hamlet by the Royal Shakespeare Company.

I also enjoy taking a variety of college courses. I think everything you learn helps you become a more believable writer.

Sharon Gagon

The Perfect Escape

Once again I find myself, in a search for solace, driving toward Bolsa Chica Beach. Since I was a kid, I've escaped there whenever my fragile psyche felt threatened. Before I know it, I'm sitting in near meditation, on the sand. The tide has gone out, the sand is still moist. It breaks into pieces as I burrow my feet below. The people fade away. The cars, the apartments, everything disappears. I am alone. I bury myself deeper. I become part of the sand, I am part of the earth. For a time, I am immortal.

I've often come to this personal haven. Sometimes mindlessly, not even remembering how I got there. I was just there with the welcome sound of the waves, the seagulls circling tirelessly, melding with the sand.

I spent a lot of time here as a kid. My father would bring me and my little brother, Chris, with only the slightest urging. My mother, on the other hand, was an entirely different story. There are two kinds of people in this world, "beach people" and "non-beach people." My mother was a classic "non-beach" person. A picnic at the beach? "I can just throw sand in my sandwich at home, thank you very much." So we'd leave her at home in her bathrobe kept company by her Life Magazine and Final Jeopardy. My dad was one of "us." He was always ready to throw a sandchair, a cooler and us kids in the car and head west. Chris and I would spend hours, sometimes days, running along the water's edge playing "the waves can't get me," speckled with salt and seaspray, sand in every imaginable crevice. We were kids; we didn't care. We didn't even mind the sand in our bologna sandwiches; it was just extra crunch.

At first the water would seem terribly cold, but as we slowly worked our way out, it felt warm around us. I loved to play jump the waves. The ground disappearing under my feet, floating over the crest of the wave, soaring over the crest, then landing back on earth. If the wave was too big, Chris would call out, "Go under," but I hated going under. As Chris submerged, letting the wave pass harmlessly over his head, I still had to try to jump it. Sometimes I'd make it. Other times I'd be caught in the wave and spin uncontrollably through the white, foamy water, tumbling through the small rocks, sand and seaweed before being deposited, coughing, on the shore. I'd sit on the sand, with salty tears, contemplating the error of my judgment. Eventually getting all the sand and salt water out of my nose and throat, I'd promise myself, next time I'll go under.

Some days my Dad would scoop me up and carry me out, way past the breakers, further than I'd ever dare venture on my own. Usually there was nobody else out there so, in a sense, we had the ocean to ourselves. Sometimes he'd pretend to be falling or drop me. He never fooled me, I never was scared. I felt so safe, so secure in his arms, I never believed he could let me go.

Sand and kids, they were made for each other. The pleasure we'd derive, the imagination we'd show. Your first sandcastle or the first time your moat filled with water without destroying the castle, you stand amazed at your architectural accomplishment. With our buckets and shovels and whatever makeshift tools we picked up along the way, we could build anything. Some days it was castles, sometimes it was volcanoes, and once, in fourth grade, we even made a California mission.

I remember I was about five years old when I asked my Dad if we could go to the beach so I could play with the sandcastle I'd made last week. Oh, the innocence and naivete of youth. My father had to explain to me that my castle wasn't there anymore. It would have been washed away by the pounding surf by now (or kicked down by some other kid). I was pretty upset. I'd spent a lot of time and effort on that castle. It was like my best one ever. Dad tried to comfort me. He said it wasn't that my sandcastle was gone, it was just different. All the pieces were still there, just in another shape. He said that next time I could make my castle again or make something else with the same sand. I could make anything I wanted, and, in some form, it would always be there for me.

It was far too profound for a five year old to appreciate, but Dad was doing the best he could. My Dad. . . .

When I was thirteen I walked the four miles from our housing tract looking for comfort at this familiar beach, driven there by my first broken heart. I was so in love with Bobby Morton, at least as deeply in love as a thirteen year old can be. I was unceremoniously dumped for Kim Forest. I couldn't believe it! Kim Forest, the blonde bimbo from English class. Kim Forest, who couldn't tell a noun from a verb if you put a gun to her head. Who once spelled "Cleveland National Forrest" wrong, even though Forest was her last name. The same Kim Forest who, during Literature, said that Shakespeare was "so cool, he could write for television." Her sole claim to fame was a size 34B. In eighth grade, that was more than enough to take away anyone's boyfriend. The thought of having to face people at school was more than I could bear. The fear of coming around a corner and running into her, into them (her 34B's, I mean) was more than any thirteen year old, even a very mature one like myself, should have to endure. The answer seemed obvious; I would simply have to quit school. It wasn't what I wanted, but I could see no other way. I sat and stared out at the horizon. Throwing aside some dried up seaweed, I laid back, not worrying about the sandy mess I was making of my long brown hair. I don't know how long I lay there, it could have been an hour, it could have been five minutes. I lost contact with time. This was the first time it happened, the first time I became part of the sand. I was overwhelmed by the enormity of it all; the powerful waves, the setting sun, our whole cosmic environment. It made me feel very small, but it made Bobby Morton and Kim Forest seem even smaller, less important. Surrounded by this grandeur, the two of them were inconsequential. They were nothing. I was almost smug when I left the beach that day. I was ready for them, ready to show off my new-found strength.

Bobby Morton did come crawling back to me after three weeks with little Ms. IQ, but by then it was too late. I had moved on to bigger and better things, namely Davey Roberts. It did feel good to turn Bobby down.

When I turned sixteen and my parents became the most unreasonable people on earth, I really needed the solitude of the beach. It was somewhere I could go to escape the pressure, the demands, the rules. It was somewhere I could go to get away from my parents' voices. They were disappointed with my biology grade, they didn't like my choice of friends, they didn't understand my attitude. Why did they expect me to be perfect? Whether it was grades, or boys, or staying out after curfew, they were always disappointed and hurt. I was always the bad guy.

My escape was driving up Pacific Coast Highway, turning at the Jack in the Box on the corner, hoping for a free park, and finally collapsing in the sand. Safety.

The ocean is an amazing thing, a paradox, really. It's simple, yet complex. It's constantly changing, but it's always the same. This was never so obvious to me as when I took my first photography class at Golden West College. We spent the first few weeks getting a grip on the basics; understanding the significance of F-stops, shutter speed, and film type. Fumbling in the darkness, painstakingly winding the film on the reel, not knowing whether you've destroyed your "masterpieces" until the process was completed. Once I had gotten through all the required technical assignments, I was set free. Free to capture my favorite subject on film. My photo class was a great excuse to spend hours at the beach. I could go to the same spot, same time of day, even use the same camera and lens, but I never captured the same shot twice. Each photo was unique. Subtle differences, obvious differences, there were always differences. A deserted sandcastle marked the landscape one day, vanished the next. A lone seagull, or a flock of seagulls, sometimes an empty sky. Tire tracks from the lifeguard's jeep, glaring evidence of human intrusion, slowly disappearing as the beach healed itself.

As the photographs piled up, like mounting evidence, I found a new appreciation for the beach. It had, for me, new life.

It was at a computer workshop at Golden West College that I met David. He was tall, blonde and had the remnants of a summer tan. He worked in Irvine and, like myself, was trying to become more computer literate. We hit it off right away. It was over coffee during a class break that he asked me out. When he suggested we go to the beach for our first date, I got chills. I took it as a serious sign. When he told me he surfed, I just knew he had it too, that beach thing.

Our day at the beach was perfect. It was hot, with a nice ocean breeze to make it just right. David packed a great picnic lunch. We ate, we laughed, we built sand castles, we played footprint games in the sand. Mostly, we just shared. I lay in his arms as the sun slowly set and felt that I'd found someone who was going to be a very important part of my life.

My parents loved him. He said his parents loved me, but I was never quite sure about his mother. I would catch her staring when she thought no one would notice, and I can't say that her face was filled with love or approval. But despite what David called "my imagination," things were wonderful between us. We saw each other constantly. It was on Valentine's Day that he took me to our special spot on the beach and told me he wanted to spend the rest of his life with me. Down on one knee, he slipped the diamond ring on my finger. The ring was beautiful, the night was beautiful. I was just certain that our life together was going to be beautiful.

Life is full of ups and downs. What I don't understand is why the ups are followed so closely by the downs. I had barely begun the wedding plans when David started back-peddling. He got scared, or something. Afraid of the commitment, the responsibility, being tied down, I don't know what. Maybe he met Kimberly Forest. Whatever his problem was, things deteriorated quickly. I gave him his ring back; I couldn't stand to watch him squirm anymore. He left with the requisite promises. He was confused, but he still loved me. He needed some time, but he would call. He almost sounded like General MacArthur in his famous "I shall return" speech. Meanwhile, as the door closed behind him, I knew he was not coming back. I knew that was the end of "our beautiful life together."

I just felt empty. I wanted to run for comfort to the beach, but I couldn't. This was where we had laughed and played. This is where I fell in love with him. This is where I agreed to be his wife. How could I go there to forget him? I was angry with him for hurting me, and I was even more angry that he'd taken my special place away.

I, of course, could not abandon the beach forever. It was too much a part of me. With a little time, and a little distance from David, I could find more than just painful memories along the water's edge. I still cringed when I saw lovers walking hand in hand at the shoreline. Sometimes the footprints they left in the wet sand would cause my throat to tighten and my eyes to blur. I still caught myself staring at blossoming love with a mixture of resentment and nostalgia. But I could see past it too. I could see the life and the beauty, I could taste the salt air, I could feel the warmth and security. I could feel "right" again.

The beach is a different place to everyone. For children, it's a magical playland. For teenagers, it's an escape or a place to be loud and not get thrown out. It can be a place to fall in love, a place to escape the heat, or just a place to get a tan. At different times in my life, it's been all of these. But not today. Today I'm not here because of a school girl crush, misguided love, or a need for entertainment. Today I'm not here to build sandcastles.

Today is different.

Today, we buried my father.

People said it was a lovely funeral; I don't know what that means. A blur of nameless, faceless people streamed by. He looks so natural, they'd say. Did they actually look at him, I had wondered. How could they even mutter that tired, ridiculous cliche if they had really looked at him. He was so pale, so cold, and so painfully still. It was all so unnatural. He was only fifty-two. Fathers aren't supposed to die at fifty-two. They're supposed to get old and eventually retire; they're supposed to give you away at your wedding; they're supposed to become grandfathers; and they're supposed to teach their grandchildren how to build sandcastles. They're supposed to do all those things. They are not supposed to get cancer and die at fifty-two.

I should be home, I suppose, but the house was so full of relatives and well-meaning friends. The noise, the confusion, I couldn't even think. But here, without the noise and confusion, I realize just how much thinking hurts.

I just don't understand. I want to make sense of it, but I can't. The sun came up this morning at its prescribed time, the waves continue to beat methodically on the shore, and my father's dead. What sense can it make?

Maybe it is like my father said about my sandcastle, that it wasn't really gone, just different. That it would always be there in some shape or form. I can't accept he's just gone and that it's over. There has to be more. I have to believe he's still here, just in some other way. That, just like the sand on the beach, he'll always be there for me. And there's nowhere I could feel closer to him than on this beach.

Maybe I will build a sandcastle after all.

Anne

Betty M. Farrell
Laguna Hills

I am a single parent of an adult daughter and a teen-age son. We moved to Orange county from Memphis, Tennessee, thirteen years ago and I've felt at home here from the first day.

My mother is a published author and her grandfather and uncle owned small-town newspapers. I learned to read when I was five years old, and I've always felt stories inside me demanding to escape. It wasn't until fall, 1993, that I finally risked letting them out.

This particular story, "Anne", was inspired by a woman I met in 1987 at Saddleback College. She was a bright, articulate woman working toward her second degree and with a promising new career. Unanticipated changes resulted in her living in her car for six months. I admired the courage she portrayed in acknowledging her problem, in reaching out for help, and in graciously accepting that help. As a nearly divorced mom, I was paralyzed by the fear of poverty and homelessness. This woman's story persuaded me that it was not shameful to ask for help, that from time to time we all need assistance, and we need to offer each other aid.

I specifically chose South Orange County for the setting of my story because I believe the homeless are less visible here than North Orange County, for example, and I wanted to applaud one of the many organizations, and their volunteers, that reach out to help.

Betty M. Farrell

Anne

The Cal-Trans truck rocked gently as its left tires rolled up on the curb and out of the traffic. The driver set the emergency brake and flipped on the hazard lights. He and his two co-workers climbed out in the dark morning, switched on their powerful flashlights, and slid through the bougainvillea and loose dirt that covered the hillside above I-5 and Avenida Pico.

Anne jerked awake and tightened her grip on the rusty dinner knife.

"Someone's coming!" she whispered to her companion sleeping nearby. He didn't stir. She shivered in the early morning chill and waited. Whoever's trampling through the brush makes enough noise to wake the dead, Anne thought. She wiggled her freezing toes and strained to see in the gray dawn.

Suddenly a bright light lit up the clearing. Anne shaded her eyes with a corner of the ragged blanket and clutched the knife handle to her chest.

"Wake up!" she hissed, "Wake up!"

Her companion didn't answer.

"Hey," a voice yelled from behind the light, "I see some down here."

Anne heard more heavy footsteps. The light stopped in front of her and a gravelly voice shouted, "Get up! Ya' gotta' move." The toe of a work boot swung at Anne's head and her knife flashed from beneath the blanket. It slashed at the metal toe with a dull CLANK. The foot and the light withdrew a step.

"Be careful, boys," the growly voice said. "This one's armed."

Several male voices snickered.

Anne wondered why Luke didn't at least roll over to complain about the noise. Maybe he's too hungover, she thought. Her own head felt like it was caught in a vise, and her body ached from sleeping on the cold ground. She peeked out from the blanket.

The lantern and the early morning light showed her three strangers dressed in orange jumpsuits walking among the sleepy figures on the hillside. One of the intruders poked at Luke a few times with his toe; then he stooped down for a closer look. He lifted a corner of the mud-stained covering and reached under it hesitantly. His face sagged with weariness, and he bit his lower lip. He looked sadly at Anne, still huddled in her blanket.

"Do you know this man?" he asked.

48

"Why?"

"Do you know his name?"

"Why should I tell you?"

"Because he's dead."

"No. He's just drunk."

"No. He's dead."

Her tears surprised her.

The man rose and stepped around Luke's body. He stood over Anne and repeated his question, "Do you know his name?"

"Luke," she said in a hushed voice.

He pulled a notebook and pencil from his jumpsuit pocket.

"Luke what?"

"I don't know."

"How long have you known him?"

"I don't know."

"Was it a few days? Weeks? Months?"

"I don't know! I don't know!" Anne moaned. Her head throbbed, and she wished this man would shut up.

"What's your name?"

Anne tensed. "Why?" she asked, eyeing him suspiciously.

"I need to know, for my report."

"I don't . . ."

"Just your first name, then. So I'll know what to call you." His gravelly voice sounded gentler.

"Anne," she murmured.

"Okay, Annie, ..."

"It's Anne!" she stressed impatiently.

"Okay. Anne."

He knelt in the dirt beside her and shifted his CAL-TRANS hat farther back on his head.

"I'm Robert," he said, "but most people call me Bud." He drawled the 'B-u-u-d.'

Anne smiled without meaning to.

"Hey, Bud," a voice yelled from the slope behind them, "we got most of 'em packed up and movin' on. Ya' want help with those two?"

"I'll take care of it," Bud called back to his co-worker. "You need to move on, too," he told Anne, "The county is cleaning up all the freeway underpasses this week."

Cleaning up, thought Anne, as if we were trash. She sighed long and deep, and began to unravel herself from the blankets. The knife slipped from her hand and tumbled softly to the dirt. She snatched it up and held it protectively in her right hand while she gathered her few possessions with her left. Bud watched her silently.

"Where will you go?" he asked.

"What do you care?"

"I don't know. You don't seem like most of the homeless I see. You seem more ... I don't know ... you don't seem like you belong here."

Anne stood and stared Bud in the eyes.

"None of us belongs here."

She gave Luke's still form a long, sad look. Bending, she gently stroked his exposed foot.

"Bye, Luke. I'll miss you," she whispered. She turned and followed the others.

Anne stumbled through the bushes up to the road. A few trucks and cars whizzed past her as the drivers hurried toward the I-5. Anne walked aimlessly along the edge of Avenida Pico, lost in her thoughts. None of us belong here; none of us belong here. I don't even know where I belong. Anne sighed and brushed her wet eyes with the back of her hand, leaving gritty brown streaks across her cheeks. Her sandals slapped softly on the pavement, occasionally flicking a small stone under her heel. She barely noticed. She gripped the tattered wool blanket with grimy fingers. Horns blared when Anne stepped into the intersection at El Camino Real. Lifting her eyes she saw the ocean in the distance, nearly hidden in the mist. On her right was a familiar-looking house. Anne pressed her fingers to her temples trying to remember when she had been here before. The memory was too elusive. A sign over the front door read, EPISCOPAL SERVICES ALLIANCE. WELCOME.

Anne searched for the cleanest section of the blanket and scrubbed her face and hands. She took a deep breath and stepped uncertainly up to the door. When she reached the threshold the aroma of coffee filled her lungs. She sagged against the doorjamb and sniffed the air.

A woman, carrying a steaming mug, approached Anne.

"Can I help you?" She sipped from the mug.

"Yes . . . No . . . Do you have food here?"

"Just coffee and donuts. The food bank is around the corner. Are you all right?"

"I need help." Anne blurted.

"Come. My name's Melissa. I'm a counselor here."

Anne followed Melissa into a tiny office. Crammed into the room was a small metal desk, burdened with stacks of folders, books, and note pads. A short metal file cabinet held a coffeemaker and an opened box of donuts.

"I know it's a mess. I'm just getting settled." Melissa said.

She pointed to one of the two folding chairs and poured steaming coffee into a bright yellow mug adorned with a smiling face. She lifted the donut box, turned to Anne, and extended her arm.

Anne raised a chocolate covered donut to her lips and savored the almost forgotten sweetness. She gulped the scalding coffee, burning her tongue and upper lip.

"Ouch!"

"Careful."

"It'll be okay."

Melissa sat in the second chair, facing Anne.

"Have you been here before?"

"I don't ... I don't think so."

"You don't remember?"

Anne shook her head.

"What's your name?"

"Anne. I think."

"You don't know?"

"No."

"Why do you think its Anne?"

Anne reached inside her jacket, unzipped a small pocket and retrieved a delicate gold bracelet, with the name ANNE, suspended by gold links. She laid it daintily on her dirt-streaked palm.

"This was in the jacket."

"Where did you get the jacket?"

"When I woke up in the alley, I was cold and looked for something to wrap up in. It was lying in a heap under me. I put it on."

"Why were you in an alley?"

"Don't know." Anne shook her head and slipped the bracelet back into the pocket. She picked at her broken fingernails.

"What did you do then?"

Anne took a deep breath.

"Wandered out to the street. Saw a line of people. Got in line. Some people were handing out coffee and sandwiches behind a church. So I got something to eat. I sat at a bus stop for a long time. Tried to figure out who I was and what I was supposed to be doing."

"Did you look for help? The police?"

"Yes. I saw two policemen, at the bus stop. I tried to ask, but one waved his nightstick and said, 'Move on!'" Anne motioned with her hand. "The other one stood with his thumbs in his belt and glared at me.

I didn't know what to say. So I went back to the alley and climbed under some empty boxes to keep warm when night came."

"Where were you before you woke up in the alley?"

"I don't remember."

"Do you remember anything?"

Anne rubbed her temples with her fingertips.

"Lights. Big, bright lights in a huge dark place. Then the alley."

"How long did you stay in the alley?"

"Days. I don't know how many."

"No one helped ou?"

"Luke." Her voice cracked. "I met him in the food line. He was old. Nearly bald. His wife had thrown him out because he drank too much. He did drink too much. But he was gentle, and patted my hand. Told me how to watch out for the cops and where there were other places to get food. I just kind of trailed after him after that."

"What kind of help do you want, Anne?"

"I want to know who I am. Where I belong. Who I belong to."

"Why don't we try to find out what you do know."

"How?"

"I'll try to prompt your memories with some questions. Anytime you want to stop, just say so. Okay?"

"Okay."

"Let's start with the light. What do you remember about the light?"

"Two lights. Very bright. Looking at them hurt my eyes." She rubbed her eyes at the memory.

"Anything else?"

"No. Well . . . No."

"Tell me about waking up in the alley. Were you injured?"

"Oh, yes! I ached everywhere! Little pebbles poked into my back and the side of my face. My head pounded. Bruises on my arms and legs. Broken fingernails. Two of my fingers had dried blood on them.

"What about the soup kitchen? Did you ask for help there?"

"I tried to. But they were so crowded. And they just wanted us to all move through quickly."

"Do you have any other ideas about who you are? Any other clues?"

"Well, I did find something else here in the big pocket." Anne slipped her hand in and gently removed some papers. She laid them reverently on the disheveled desk so Melissa could see two small paper roses, one crayoned in pink, the other in red.

"On the back they say, 'I love you, Sarah.' I don't remember a

52

Sarah."

"Okay, Anne, Let me make some phone calls. See if we can find out something. In the meantime, would you like to take a shower, ..."

"Yes! Yes! Could I?"

"Come with me." Melissa smiled.

She took Anne's arm and led her out of the office and across a spacious entry hall. Anne heard voices in a distant room, laughing, chatting voices of people who seemed to have purpose. Did I used to be like them?

Melissa guided Anne into a room that looked like a library, but instead of books on the shelves, they were now stacked with clean-smelling clothes, socks and sneakers. Melissa helped Anne select what she needed, then they walked up a flight of stairs. At the landing Melissa nodded toward a fresh, white bathroom.

"Shower as long as you like." She said, "Here's a plastic bag for your soiled things. Enjoy. Come downstairs to my office when you're ready." She patted Anne's arm, turned, and descended.

Anne nodded. She backed into the bathroom, closed and locked the door. She faced a full-length mirror. Studying her reflection, Anne said to the face staring back, "You know who I am, don't you."

Turning her back to the door, she peeled off her dirty clothes, turned on the shower and stepped behind the curtain. Anne closed her eyes and stood under the hot spray, letting the stinging torrent massage her face and body. Her heart pounded in her ears. The lump in her throat threatened to choke her.

"I see the lights. Two bright lights. I see them! Behind me?"

Opening her eyes, she twisted her head sharply to the right and looked behind her.

"It's just a fiberglass wall." She whispered. "No. I do remember. It was a car. No. A truck. A truck followed me ... parking lot ... San Juan Depot. He bumped my car. I got out to see what ... grabbed my hair ... threw me to the pavement."

Anne twisted the knob to OFF, cast the shower curtain aside, and with fumbling fingers pulled on jeans and a T-shirt. She jerked at the door, but it wouldn't open. She pounded on it, shouting, "Let me out!" Then she remembered it was locked. Panting, she yanked the door open and dashed out, colliding with Melissa.

"What? What's the matter? Are you okay?"

"Yes! I know what the lights are!"

"What ..."

Anne opened her mouth to answer, but was interrupted by a voice shouting from below.

"Anne! Oh, my God! It's Anne!"

Footsteps pounded on the stairs. Anne gripped Melissa's arms and stared, wide-eyed, at the woman bounding toward them two steps at a time.

"Anne! It's me! Eva! Anne?"

"Eva?" Anne cocked her head to one side. "Eva? How do you know me?"

"We work here. You work here."

"I do?"

"Yes. Don't you remember? Last spring. You were going to drive one of your clients to the train station. You didn't come into work the next day, or the next. We called your house. We called the police. No one could find you. Where have you been?"

"I'm not sure myself."

Eva wrapped her arms around Anne and murmured into her ear, "Sarah will be so happy to see you."

Anne pushed herself away and searched Eva's eyes.

"Who's Sarah?"

"My little girl. You used to bring her animal stickers and take her for ice cream."

"I want to remember ... but ... it's all so ... vague." Anne slumped against Melissa.

Eva stepped into the bathroom and snatched a towel from the rack. Placing it over Anne's sopping hair, she laid her arm around Anne's shoulders, giving her a squeeze. "Let's go down to Melissa's office and get a cup of coffee ... and talk."

I do belong, thought Anne, as they descended the stairs. I do belong somewhere. I am Anne.

The Old Man

Greta Macias
Seal Beach

Best wishes!
Greta Macias

Orange County is Southern California, and it is not. It is small town and big city, and it is country and wide open spaces. It is beach; it is desert. It is play, and it is hard work. It is crystal cathedral, and it is boozing at the beach. It is john birch conservative and laguna beach liberal. It is very rich and it is very poor. It is country club and it is homelessness. It is freeway and country lane. It is the shopping mall and the mom and pop store. It is crafts and art and symphony concerts - and it is line dancing, progressive jazz and coffee houses - and it is the boom box and the neighbor kid who practices rock and roll in the garage. It is youth roller blading on the street, and it is retirement communities with swimming pools and golf courses. It is cultural diversity, and it is not cultural diversity. It was once a place of orange groves and ranches; it is now a place of industry and financial palaces.

The aerospace industry, a large part of which exists in Orange County, is a fascinating part of the life here, and I was fortunate to have worked in it for thirteen years. The people who work or have worked in it have interesting stories to tell - but, mostly, these stories have not been told to the outside world. I am pleased to share a little slice of that world in this story.

Greta Macias

The Old Man

It seemed inevitable since I live in Orange County that I would one day work for the aerospace industry. And with it, my life took on the peculiar waxings and wanings of the ups and downs of military budgets. Lots of money from the Department of Defense meant lots of people working. The parking lots were full. There were lots of new hires. I remember some of them with vivid clarity....

His name was Adolf Martin but no one ever called him Adolf. Everyone had too much respect for him and the business from the war to call him Adolf. You either said Mr. Martin or you called him "Al". I always said Mr. Martin.

The company had been forced to retire him on his 65th birthday. That was the law in the State of California then and The Company had to conform to the law. But Mr. Martin didn't retire. He only accepted the going-away-party, the gifts from friends as well as the good wishes.... And he came back. I don't know how he got around Security. He had worked in a "Black Box" area and security was extremely tight. Because he had a Retiree badge, he could come and go into the areas that were unclassified: the library, Employee Services, the auditorium when there were unclassified presentations. He taught a class after hours in photography to any employees who were interested, using one of the unclassified conference rooms. But, of course, he was doing more than that. And it had to take collusion on the part of several people to make it happen. Security was tight.

On the books, Mr. Martin was classified as an optics engineer, but he would have been better described as a highly knowledgeable optics technician. He was one of a few who understand super sensitivity lenses and film, plus the whole array of equipment that allows us to photograph objects on the ground from a vehicle in space. He wasn't really an engineer by training, and I never knew how he had been able to parlay his knowledge of photography into the intricacies of space optics. But he had and he was well respected.

I first met him a few weeks after I came to work for The Company. I was the Personnel Manager and among many duties, I recruited and hired engineers and scientists for various space projects. One of the Directors asked that I prepare an offer of employment for a Mr. Adolph Martin. He said that Al was a former employee and I could get his file out of Records for any information I needed to prepare the offer. Sixty-five was no longer mandatory retirement age.

I worked up the best possible salary offer I could. I allowed for the increase in the cost of living for the five years that he had been retired, which was a pretty generous thing to do. After all, the records showed that he had not worked for five years, so he now had the same number of years of experience as when he had left the Company.... But technological advances in the fast paced world of space optics would have put him behind the salary curve by five years... not to mention a possible loss of his own skills during five years of disuse.

When I took the offer sheet to the Director for his signature, he objected to the money. "You haven't figured in the years that Al has been working here since he retired." That was certainly news to me as there was no record anywhere that there had been further experience, much less with The Company. But Mr. Martin had worked approximately 25 to 32 hours a week for The Company for the previous five years. And he hadn't been paid. As I probed deeper, I encountered a very clever and subtle stone-walling.

"Well," I replied, "in order to offer more money I'll have to show that experience and we both know I can't do that." He insisted that I prepare a second offer at a higher figure. Being new and not knowing how much real authority I had, I decided to prepare two offers. I signed the original but also sent along the second, higher one, with the director's recommendation based on the fact that he had kept his skills and knowledge current. There was no mention of additional experience. When I presented the offers to Dr. Bishop, he signed the second one immediately and asked me to destroy the original. Then, smiling most engagingly, he asked me to sign with my approval on the second one. I respectfully asked him if he understood the implications of the offer. He told me that he never signed anything without consulting with his subordinates. So..., he knew! But I was also sure that Security did not know. The lessons I had learned early in the Personnel field about sealed lips would apply doubly here, at The Company.

I called the number I had for Mr. Martin. Using an outside line and being unfamiliar with all of the numbers that came into the buildings, I thought I was calling him at home. After I identified myself, Mr. Martin said, "Wait! Wait! Don't say it now! I want to see you when you say it! Do you understand me? Don't say it yet. I'm coming to your office." Since he lived approximately 20 miles away, I set the file aside and started to work on something else.

Five minutes later, there was a strong knock on my door. I called, "Come!" and in walked this slight, dapper gentleman, brown eyes sparkling, the broadest of smiles on his face, a forehead that went round to the back of his head, shoulders squared, feathery wisps of dark brown hair around his ears, neatly trimmed moustache, chin thrust forward. The only betrayals of his age were the brown age spots on his hands and the folds of skin that had slipped over the outer corners of his eyes. His manner, his countenance, was one of youth.

He made a little courtly bow and said, "I am so happy to make your acquaintance. I am Al Martin. Please, please let me hold your hands." I got up from my chair, came around my desk, and let him take both my hands in his. Then he said, "Please look at me with your angel eyes. Now, now, you can say the magic words!" And smiling even more broadly, he pulled my hands to his breast as I said, "Mr. Martin, it gives me a great deal of pleasure to extend an offer of employment to you as a Member of the Technical Staff of The Company." .. and I mentioned a monthly salary.

"I accept! I accept! I have never been so happy! If I knew you better I would kiss both of your cheeks." And he proceeded to kiss both of my hands. Then he put my hands down and, in disgust, said, "Retirement is Hell!"

He signed the papers, bowed in his courtly fashion, and was gone.

Months later, I stepped off the elevator on the second floor, late, and in a rush to a meeting... when I stopped abruptly. Lining the walls of the reception area of this floor and up and down both sides of the long halls was a display of photographs that were arresting. I was particularly struck by one of an old woman whose face showed so much suffering, pain, sorrow, anguish, despair as she sat on a park bench in what appeared to be a European setting. I promised myself that I would see them at the first available moment.

As soon as I could, I was back to see the photos. They were in sepia and black and white. The one of the old woman was labeled only with the date and place it had been taken: Berlin, 1936. And that told the whole story. All of the photographs were dated before 1938. One of the latest was of the Statue of Liberty, rising grandly out of a mist, taken in 1937. The pictures covered a period of ten years and showed people in all stages of living. The photographer had captured all the subtleties of emotion from pathos to joy, fear, anger, love, hate, self-righteousness, pomposity, disdain, holiness, adoration, contempt, mockery, mischief, lust, greed, hope, generosity, trust, wistfulness, weariness, pain. The pictures were the most sensitive photos I had ever seen. The body language and the faces were exquisite. They were incredible works of art. Now, fifteen years later, I can still recall many of them. My favorite was of a baby of, perhaps, seven months smiling a smile of unbridled glee as he reached for his mother's ready breast. The people were so alive. It was a most remarkable display. There was a small sign at the end that said, "Ten years of life... Al Martin".

I arranged to have lunch with Mr. Martin in the cafeteria and was pleased when he walked towards me across the eating area with his tray in hand. I wanted to know more about this man who wore his passions so close to his skin. He was smiling broadly and made his courtly bow to me before he sat down. He always wore a newsboy's style cap when he had to walk in the sun, and he set this aside with a flourish. "You give me so much pleasure", he said in his formal and slightly accented English, "to ask an old man to have lunch with you. But that is the reason I love to work here so much. Here, the nice young people all say, 'Good morning, Mr. Martin. How are you, Mr. Martin? Good to see you, Mr. Martin.' Here, there is respect for me. I am known and even liked by so many people."

He went on to tell me that in the first weeks of his retirement, he had stayed home and after so many days and hours, his wife had suggested he might take a walk in the park... and plan to stay the afternoon. He did. And the only people he saw there were the young nannies and young mothers with small children. When he had tried to smile and touch the children, the women usually pulled their children away. He was devastated. He sometimes saw older people, too, but they seemed to be lost in a world of remembrance and were not interested in being disturbed by another old man. He said, "I told you retirement was Hell."

Over the nine years that I stayed at The Company, I eventually worked in the same building with Mr. Martin and, quite often, we encountered each other at meetings or in the hall or had lunch together in the Cafeteria. We had become friends in a most wonderful way: warm, interested, always professional and never very personal. He was vibrantly enthusiastic about the life going on around him at that moment. If we passed each other in the hall, he turned his smile up to full wattage. In mid-stride, he managed a half-bow in my direction. He made me feel that my mere presence improved his already wonderful day.

Mr. Martin was a rare experience within the fortified walls of The Company. Our employees were principally engineers and scientists, brilliance was the norm, and for most of their lives, they had majored in things, not feelings, not emotions. The strength that I brought to them was my ability to see beyond thing problems and assist them with the human issues that did not lend themselves to resolution on a computer. I did my job well. I learned to speak their language as if it were my mother tongue. But, personally, I often felt quite isolated. I occasionally needed some one to interact with who could speak my language to me. Because of Mr. Martin's sensitivity, his ability to see, really see the people around him, his willingness to live so completely in the moment, I found great comfort being with him... even though we never shared our private, more personal lives with each other.

One day he came by my office wearing his usual jaunty attitude and, even though I had plenty of work to do, I went with him because he asked me to. When we got to the inner patio in the South wing of our building, he took my hand and almost on tiptoe, his finger to his lips, he led me to the base of a young tree and pointed upwards to a branch about seven feet off the ground. Hidden in the leaves, so that I almost could not see it even though he was directing my attention to it, there was a tiny humming bird nest and protruding out of the little hole that was its doorway was the needle nose of the mother bird. We stood as still as statues, barely breathing, and waited. After a few minutes, the brightly colored papa brought the mama a bite of bug or nectar, we couldn't tell, and then he flew away.

What an eye for beauty, what patience, our Mr. Martin had. And he had shared it only with me. I felt so touched and so honored. We went back to that spot together several times, waiting for the babies to be born. But Mr. Martin had said from the beginning that the parents weren't too smart... bird brains, after all. He warned me that the little branch was precarious and he turned out to be right again. A bad wind storm howled and slammed through the night. The next morning, as I drove down Orangethorpe, I saw sturdy branches and palm fronds, roof shingles and other detritus littering the ground. Mr. Martin was waiting for me. We checked the nest. But it wasn't there anymore. It was just gone. There was no wreckage. It had disappeared. We sadly went to have a cup of coffee together, toasted the two love birds and wished them well.

Weeks later, Mr. Martin was at my door. He had something to show me... a stack of paper that was about 30 inches square and an inch high. The picture on top was mostly blackness with clusters of white pinpoints. "Do you know what this is?" he asked. It was the entire continent of Europe at about one o'clock in the morning. Then he showed me the same view at midnight, at eleven, at ten, and at nine,

61

each new photo showing more pinpoints of light. "I heard you are planning to retire. Why, why, why? Here, you are a star. See how little you can become? These clusters of light are whole cities. I hear you are planning to live in Vienna for awhile. This is Vienna, here. You will be lost. Not even a pinpoint. Don't do it, Gretchen." He only called me Gretchen when he was upset. It means little Greta. As I am taller than he is, it always struck me a little humorously. But I wasn't particularly delighted at that moment to find that my advance plans for retirement had made it through the rumor mill. The pictures were amazing, though. I avoided responding to Mr. Martin's dismay and asked if he had any similar photos of the United States that I might see. Yes, there were some in the stack, also.

"This must be Los Angeles... even Orange County," I said. Yes, I was right. "Which little pinpoint way, way down there do you think I am now, Mr. Martin?" But, he protested, if I stood right there in front of him, he wouldn't have to think of me as a pinpoint in a picture. I tried to make the moment a little lighter and reminded him that I wasn't going to leave for over a year. He gave me his courtly bow as he turned to leave.

Once a year, all employees in The Company, in concert with their managers, are required to do a "Performance Evaluation" of themselves. These are completed prior to the salary plan which determines how much money each person earns for the coming year. I read Mr. Martin's evaluation. His manager noted that Mr. Martin had begun to slow down in the general quantity of his work. I was startled at this criticism, even though I knew that he was now seventy-nine.

It was then that I learned from the manager about the death of Mr. Martin's first wife and his subsequent escape through Romania. He had somehow managed to get into the United States, a very difficult thing for Jews fleeing Europe at that time. It was several years before he let anyone get close enough for him to fall in love again. And then, more years passed before they were able to have children. Their only child, a son, was about thirty-three years old now, and he was retarded. He lived at home with Mr. and Mrs. Martin.

I didn't hear much more about Mr. Martin for a few months, and he hadn't stopped to see me for a long time. I was told by one of his colleagues that he was burning a lot of midnight oil, working on a project he was very excited about.

Six weeks later, I got word there was going to be a reception for four of our engineers in our executive conference room. The General Manager's secretary would see to it that there was a cake and coffee for twenty-five, and I put it on my calendar. The Air Force people would be making a special presentation to some of our staff in recognition of a special project that had achieved spectacular results. As I was busy with other things, I didn't really check out what or who the presentation was for. This one brought some very high brass from the Air Force and our Group Vice President. The star performers filed in and one of the four was Al Martin. He was beaming but behaving in what he considered appropriately humble fashion. Well, I thought, I guess there'll be a raise after all. And, that's what happened.

He came to see me some weeks later, just prior to taking a long and well earned vacation.

"Gretchen", he said, "when I get back from vacation, you'll be winding down and I probably won't get to see you alone before all of the hoopla they'll have for your retirement. I just wanted to say that I am very sorry you are leaving. I will miss you. And you are too young to retire."

"But, Mr. Martin," I protested, "I heard you were going to retire pretty soon, too."

"Nonsense," he said. "That's that young fellow's idea, my manager. I showed him I can still do a competent job, didn't I? When I go, they will have to carry me out of here, feet first. There's enough gasoline in my tank to last awhile, yet." He came around to my side of the desk, took my hands in his and kissed them. Then he kissed me on both cheeks. "I think you are making a mistake. But I wish you well with your plans. Remember, I already warned you: Retirement is Hell!"

I retired. And, sometimes, I think about my former colleagues at The Company with feelings of nostalgia and curiosity. I remember Al Martin very clearly.

He had a profound ability to understand, to see, and to predict, especially about his own life. But I've already said that he was a sensitive man. His solution to life's problems was to try to keep everything the way it was. I admired that... partly, I suppose, because it gave me an opportunity to know this remarkable man and to share his vision of beauty and of life. He did exactly what he needed to do for himself in order to keep his visions, his perspective, and his sense of his own self-worth, whole and alive. He loved his work.

I called The Company a few weeks ago to chat and to get an update on what is happening there... and learned that Mr. Martin had experienced a heart attack while he was working in the lab about a year ago. They had to get an ambulance and then bring a stretcher into the lab to carry him out. He got his wish. At his request, he was carried out, feet first. He died a few months later at home.... He was eighty-four years old.

The Attic

Lou Ayala
Garden Grove

As a child growing up in the South Bay area of Southern California, I looked at the county of Orange with a sense of wonder. The landscape was covered with orange trees, farms and amusement parks. While Disneyland and Knott's are still here, the farms and orchards have all but given way to homes and industry. Agriculture has been replaced with people, along with buildings to house them and their business ventures. The rolling hills have been transformed into view lots. The bean fields into business parks. Although there is now little room left for agriculture, something new is being cultivated here.

A market for culture is growing. People here in Orange County do not want to depend on Los Angeles to fill their cultural fruit basket. Whether talking about words on paper, paint on canvas or actors on stage, the arts are blossoming in Orange County, as evidenced by this harvest of work, Slices of Orange.

The setting for my contribution comes from the townhouse I recently purchased in Garden Grove. "The Attic" is a real part of my new home, though the family described in the story does not exist.

Living alone in a new home presents its own set of challenges. The house itself becomes your new constant companion. Normal house sounds (timbers expanding or contracting, birds on the roof, neighbors coming and going), become inspiration for a myriad of horrors. Ideas for stories, especially the bizarre, tend to form very easily in this type of environment. Such was the case when the idea for the following story came to mind, and I am very happy it was selected to be part of this collection.

Lou Ayala

The Attic

"What are those doors up there for, Daddy?" nine year-old Natalie asked pointing to a pair of small doors above the upstairs hallway.

"Just the attic." Paul replied without a second thought.

Natalie continued her inquiry, "Is there anything up there?"

"Nothing but a few spiders...and a place to keep little girls who ask too many questions!" he smirked as he grabbed Natalie and lifted her toward the attic. His daughter shrieked happily as he tickled her before setting her down on the floor. Paul paused to look at the attic doors. He hadn't actually been up there yet, but he planned to explore it soon. It was rather a strange way to gain access to the attic. The two doors located above the laundry area opened outward, but gave the appearance of lending access to nothing more than a storage cabinet. Paul suddenly found himself wondering about what might be up there. How could he possibly have purchased a new home without examining every inch of the place first? Their real estate agent, Al Simmons, had described the attic during their initial viewing of the townhouse. It covered only a portion of the house, The rest was all cathedral ceilings and skylights. The attic was designed to allow for maintenance of the heating and air-conditioning ducts and although there wasn't a large area of floor space, Al was sure to point out that the ceiling was high and there was plenty of room to install storage shelves should one be so inclined.

Though he'd never actually seen THIS attic, Al knew what it was like. He had sold several houses in this particular complex over the fifteen years since it had been built, and he recognized the potential for another sale with Paul and Linda Richardson. Al's office was on the very next block of Euclid Avenue, near the town center of Garden Grove. This area of Orange County had long ago melded into and blurred its boundaries with the sprawling megalopolis of "Greater Los Angeles", but Garden Grove had somehow managed to retain hints of its small town past. Though farming had long since been relegated to a few small strawberry patches, many of the old farmhouses were still standing, giving proud testament to a long tradition of agriculture. It was one of the things Linda Richardson liked about the area, something Paul would have preferred his wife had kept to herself. Good ol' Al had picked up on her interest in old architecture right away and proceeded to point out every old farmhouse in the immediate area. Paul didn't care if he ever saw another "house with history" again, but Al was a real salesman, he knew that as long he kept Linda interested in the area, he could keep the couple interested in buying a house there.

Linda came upstairs and found her husband staring at the attic doors.

"Anything wrong, honey?"

"What?" Paul replied absent-mindedly. He had no idea why, perhaps it was just the fact he had not yet been up there, but something about the attic was beginning to bother him.

"What are you staring at?"

"Huh? Oh...nothing. Just the attic."

"Well, is something wrong? You look like you've seen a ghost!"

"No, I just had a strange feeling. It's nothing. I'm going to bring the ladder up. Do you have anything you want to get out of the way? I can stash it up in the attic."

"Are you kidding? I'd hate to haul a ladder up here every time I need something out of the attic!"

"I'm sure there's plenty of room up there. It would be a shame to waste all that storage space."

"We've just started moving in, Paul. Let's get things sorted out first."

"You're right. Let's go downstairs and get that truck unloaded!"

As the new homeowners started down the stairs, Paul's eyes were once again drawn upward toward the attic.

The next day, Linda and Natalie returned home from an afternoon of shopping at South Coast Plaza. They were anxious to show Paul the things they had purchased for their new home. But he was nowhere to be found.

"Paul!" Linda called. There was no answer.

"Natalie, see if your father's in the back yard."

Linda checked upstairs. Boxes had been rearranged, some were unpacked; Paul had obviously been busy while she and Natalie were gone. She noticed the ladder standing by the laundry area. She looked toward the attic. She considered climbing the ladder before deciding there was no need. The doors were closed. At least one door would be open if he was in the attic.

Natalie called upstairs. "He's not out back, Mom!"

"Okay, I'll be down in a minute." Linda replied with a tinge of trepidation in her voice. She checked Natalie's room before looking in the master bedroom. There was no sign of her husband.

Linda guessed he was visiting with a neighbor, since his car was

68

in the garage, and he'd left the patio door wide open. Or perhaps he'd walked to Al's office for some reason. She decided to busy herself with unpacking boxes in the master bedroom. Natalie came upstairs and helped for a short time before going to her own room to unpack some of her own things. It bothered Linda that Paul would leave the house unattended with the back door open. She waited impatiently for his return.

An hour passed, Linda was becoming very concerned. She tried to tell herself there was nothing to be worried about. An hour wasn't such a long amount of time, but she couldn't help feeling something was wrong, very wrong. The doorbell rang. Linda ran downstairs as quickly as she could.

"Paul! Is that you?" she shouted as she unlocked the front door and threw it open.

"Wish I was lucky enough to be coming home to a young thing as beautiful as you, darlin'!" Al exclaimed before noticing Linda was on the verge of tears.

"Linda, are you okay?"

"I'm fine, but I'm worried about Paul! I don't know where he is, and I'm afraid something's happened to him! I was hoping he was with you!"

"No, I haven't seen him today. I'm sure nothing's wrong. Don't you worry, he'll turn up any time now."

"This is not like him. We came home over an hour ago and the patio door was wide open. He wouldn't leave the house open like that."

"Did you check the garage?"

"Yes."

"How about the back yard?"

"Yes! Yes, of course! I've checked everywhere!"

"All right, honey, calm down, everything will be fine." Al tried to console her with a reassuring hug.

Natalie watched the scene with Al and her mother from the top of the stairs. She had never seen her mother fall apart before, and she was becoming frightened.

Natalie couldn't help thinking the worst now. What if her father had fallen or had some other type of accident while she and her mother were out shopping? He could be lying injured somewhere in the house, somewhere they hadn't thought to check before. She decided to check every nook and cranny of the house starting with her parent's room. She looked through the bathroom, checked the shower stall, nothing. She opened the door leading to the balcony, looking everywhere including over the railing to the patio below. She went back inside, opened all the closets making sure to check behind boxes, still nothing.

As she came out of the bedroom, Natalie stopped in her tracks. She hadn't paid much attention to it before, but couldn't help taking notice of it now. The ladder was standing directly below the doors leading to the attic.

"He must be at a neighbor's house." Al decided "I know most of these people. Hell, I sold them their houses! I'll just go around and knock on some doors. That nasty husband of yours will be home before you've had time to dry those tears!"

Al had reassured her slightly. She was hopeful he would find Paul and this whole nightmare would be over. As Al left to check with the neighbors. Linda suddenly thought of Natalie. She realized her little breakdown with Al was not the best thing for her daughter to have witnessed. Natalie was being extremely quiet. Linda started upstairs to check on her. As she came to the top of the stair, she found Natalie on the ladder attempting to look into the attic with a flashlight.

"What are you doing, young lady?"

"I'm looking for Daddy, but I can't see much."

The little girl could barely see above the threshold of the attic door.

"Be careful Natalie...you know, I think there's a light up there..."

Before Linda could reach the light switch, the telephone rang. She rushed toward the phone in the bedroom wondering if it could be Paul calling. As Linda reached for the phone, something reached for her daughter through the attic door.

All at once, Natalie felt a cold, powerful hand close its icy grip around her wrist. Relief momentarily swept over her as she thought she had found her father. Though she had little time to consider other possibilities, as she was being pulled into the dark attic, her relief quickly turned to dread as she realized the hand around her wrist did not belong to her father. She tried to scream for her mother but could manage only a whimper before her body slammed onto the floor of the attic.

As Linda was about to lift the phone receiver, she heard strange sounds coming from the direction of the attic.

"Natalie!" Linda screamed as she let the phone go unanswered and returned to where she'd left her daughter. "Paul! Are you up there? Natalie! What's going on?!"

Linda flipped the light switch several times, but the attic remained dark. She cautiously climbed the ladder. As soon as her eyes rose above the threshold, she felt the inescapable grip of two large, cold, hands nearly encircle her entire head. Whatever creature was attached to those evil hands, it wasted no time pulling her into the attic. Dazed, Linda found herself sitting on the attic floor. She noticed the flashlight lying within reach. She picked it up and aimed it ahead of her. She suddenly preferred darkness, but could not look away from what she saw. Her eyes were transfixed on a pile of human body parts; arms, legs, torsos. The larger of the parts appeared half-eaten. Blood was oozing from severed joints. She knew this pile was all that was left of her loved ones. She knew that she would soon join the pile in a final deadly family reunion.

"What are those doors up there for?" the prospective home buyer inquired.

"Just the attic." Al Simmons replied.

Coffee Dreams

Randy D. Freeman
Fullerton

Inspiration for my story came while sitting in the Alta Coffee Shop off Newport Boulevard in Triangle Square, which ultimately served as the setting for "Coffee Dreams". The aroma of fresh brewed coffee, the sound of many voices blended with live music, the sight of hanging ferns and finished wood, along with the taste of a home-made oatmeal cookie set my imagination in motion. The idea for the story cluttered my head for several weeks until I spotted the announcement for a contest for short stories set in Orange County.

As an English teacher who spends many hours grading essays, I sometimes need a reminder that writing means much more than knowing how to correct a sentence fragment or what makes a good thesis sentence. For me, it is a means of creation and expression that provides a lot of pleasure. The problem is finding enough time and energy to write. I have heard this is a fairly common problem among writers!

My wife and I have been married a little more than a year and currently live in Fullerton. She is a graduate student in Psychology, and I will be teaching in the fall at Whittier Christian High School in La Habra.

Randy D. Freeman

Coffee Dreams

"Let's see, Friday night... The Midnight Cowboys play original folk and rock. Music starts at 8:30. Hmmm," he muttered, sitting on the couch. "Triangle Square. That's pretty close. Well, why not. Better than sitting on my butt all night with you." Bud stared at him with that stupid look on his face. "I love you, Bud, but you're not much of a conversationalist." The dog, a big golden Labrador lay down again, sighed heavily, and closed his droopy eyes.

"You need a woman as bad as I do," he continued. "Maybe more. You've never even had a girlfriend or had... well that's my fault." The dog opened his eyes and stared accusingly in response. "You're still holding a grudge, huh? Well, if it makes you feel better, I'm being punished for it. I haven't had a date since then," he said, thinking back.

An hour later, Paul Webster, left the little house he rented near the back bay of Newport beach, and drove south down Newport Boulevard. The street was crowded as usual. He had never much liked the look of Triangle Square. In fact, as he passed the glowing red "NikeTown" sign on the dome at the front end of the square, he imagined the place full of rowdy teenagers and trendy couples.

After parking on the fourth floor of an enormous garage, he made his way back down to the first floor. The little coffee shop sat right off the boulevard, introduced by a green canopy that said, "Alta Coffee and Roasting Co." Through the glass windows, he could see the place was crowded, and he made a clicking sound with his mouth which meant he was thinking. He didn't like crowded places, but he noticed a couple in the far corner getting up to leave so he hurried in. The place had a dark stained wood floor with hanging plants and paintings of rock stars on the walls. There were fresh baked deserts behind the bar near the entrance, and, of course, the nice, warm aroma of coffee.

Weaving through the tables, he passed an older couple, the woman reading some kind of romance novel with a bare-chested man on front, and the man staring blankly at the ceiling. Two younger couples sat at another table talking with their hands wrapped around ridiculously large mugs of coffee.

"Why would anyone want to drink that much coffee," he wondered as he sat down. Nestled in a darker corner of the little place, the table suited him well. He could sit in anonymity listening to the band without having everyone's conversations buzzing in his head.

A slim, dark skinned waitress sidled up. "What can I get you?"

"Well, what kind of coffee do you have?"

She laughed. "Everything. Do you want a menu?"

"No, just a decaf coffee and one of those oatmeal cookies," Paul said.

"Just plain coffee? That's pretty boring," she said, smiling. She wore her hair cut short, like a little boy's, he thought.

"Well... thank you. I try," he said aloud. He watched her go, satisfied with the encounter. She's kind of exotic looking...Indian or...Arabian. Yes, that sounds better, he thought.

He allowed himself to drift off into a lovely fantasy in which he delighted the Arabian girl with his witty conversation so much that she invited him to dinner. She cooked him an authentic Arabian meal, and they were just moving to the couch when the girl dropped off his coffee and cookie with a hurried "There you go" like she was one of those old skating waitresses. "Maybe later," he told himself. "Plenty of time." Anyway, the coffee was good and the cookie soft and chewy, just as he liked it.

The Midnight Cowboys turned out to be two middle-aged men and a slender, striking young woman. She had long brown hair that fell straight down her back finally stopping a few inches above her waist. To put it mildly, he was entranced. Watching her tune her guitar and converse with the two men was enough to satisfy him. But when they finally began to play, his pleasure rose to a new level. There was no introduction or warning when they began. One of the men, with hair receding back from his forehead but spilling out from the back onto his shoulders, played the flute. The other, a bit older and taller, played the bass, with a hunched-over, subdued style fitting for the instrument. The woman played acoustic guitar reminding him of some sixties folk singer he could not remember the name of.

They were very good. He'd always liked the flute, and it blended beautifully with the other instruments. So he sipped his coffee and nibbled his cookie in a state just shy of euphoria. When she began singing, in a strong, sulky voice, it was the perfect complement to the music. Leaning back in his chair, his eyes fell shut and a feeling of lightness overtook him so that he felt himself to be floating into the air, in a swirling of sound, color and smell. Like a child on a merry-go-round ride, he went round and round, never wanting the ride to end.

"They're pretty good, huh?"

The Merry-go-round stopped abruptly and the dark-skinned waitress was there when he got off.

"Yah, they are," he replied, embarrassed.

"Didn't mean to interrupt. Can I get you some more coffee?"

"No thanks. If I drink any more I'll... explode." He was going to say he would be going to the bathroom all night but thought it might be tacky. 'Explode' wasn't what he had wanted to say though. She moved on to another table, and he sighed, turning his attention back to the band. The song ended to scattered but enthusiastic applause.

"Thank you," the singer said smiling. "We are the Midnight Cowboys. Don't ask me why we call ourselves that. I don't really know." She paused and said something to the bass player before continuing: "This song's called 'When I Was Young'."

The gentle melody of the flute lured him into another daydream in which he was part of the band. At first, he played the flute but that was hard to imagine so he settled for the bass guitar. They played a song together and as she sang, she looked at him, and they shared a secret, communicating without words. It was a particularly pleasing fantasy since he had always dreamed of being a musician, even though he had never played an instrument other than a recorder in elementary school, and that not very well.

When he shook off the dream, the band had stopped playing and the two men stood over by the coffee bar. The young woman fiddled with her guitar and amplifier. He stood up and walked over to the stage, surprising himself, but not wanting to think about it. He took out a couple dollars from his wallet and put them in a jar at the edge of the stage.

She looked up and smiled. "Thanks."

He notice her eyes were a hazel color. "I like your music a lot.... Do you have a tape or a C.D. or something?"

"Oh, yah... somewhere." She pulled her hair back with both hands and looked around the stage. "You know what? I left them in my car. Are you leaving right now?"

"I was going to, yes, but..."

"Well, I'll run out and get them if you want. I need to get them anyway."

"Sure, no problem."

"I'll be right back," she said and then paused. "Or if you're going out you can go with me.

"Yah, sure," he said coolly while inside adrenaline pumped madly. He searched for intelligent things to say while he followed her out.

"I'm kind of afraid of parking garages at night," she confessed sheepishly when they got outside. "I watch too many movies I guess."

"I don't blame you. You never know." He scolded himself for relying on a stupid cliché. They walked up a flight of stairs and onto the second floor of the garage.

"Well, it's nice to know that some people like us. Sometimes I wonder if anyone really cares much... that people just want us to shut up so they can have a conversation."

"Really? You seem so confident up there."

She shook her head. "Well, don't tell anyone but... Where's my car?" She stopped and looked around. "Oh, there it is." Leaving the thought unfinished, she led him to a burgundy Camry and opened the trunk. She took a tape out of a box and handed it to him. On the cover, she posed with hands draped over her guitar, the two men behind her. "Like background scenery," he thought.

"Wow, looks very professional. I mean... not that you aren't professionals," he sputtered.

She raised her eyebrows and put her hands on her hips.

"I didn't mean..."

"I was going to give that to you but now...," she said playfully.

"Well, it's a little late now. You already gave it to me." Paul folded his arms in mock defiance. She made a quick grab for the tape, giggling as he held it away and brushed up against him, her hair sweeping lightly across his arm.

At the same moment, both remembered that they were strangers, and she stepped back. There was an awkward silence and then suddenly she said, "Oh shoot, I have to get back." Another pause followed. Thoughts collided in his head as he realized the significance of the moment. She misread the hesitation and made a movement to leave.

"I didn't pay for the tape," he blurted out.

"Oh, don't worry about it. We're giving some away as a promotional thing." She began walking away as she talked. "It was nice meeting you."

He made a desperate grab. "Where do you play next?"

She turned again and stopped a moment. "We're down at the Renaissance Cafe in Laguna next weekend."

"Maybe I'll see you there?"

"Maybe," she said and hurried away. A powerful urge to run after her, grab her and tell her he wanted to see her again rushed over him. But he found that he couldn't do it, and his thoughts berated him in a flood. "God, how could I blow that," he said aloud, still standing by the empty parking space. "All you had to do was ask. Why is that so hard?"

Headlights illuminated his pitiful figure, enlarging it against the wall behind the parking space. Lost in thought, his shadow stood huge and black, slightly hunched over. A gentle honk from a car startled him, and he realized the driver was waiting for him to move out of the way. Without looking up, he hurried to his car and drove home.

Once home, he sank into the couch. The dog put his head in Paul's lap, looked at him and waited. "Why am I such an wimp?" he moaned. The dog responded by putting his front legs up on the couch and licking his master's face. "Aaahhh! What are you doing, you goofy dog!" He laughed sadly. "That's the best kiss I've had in months."

He took the tape from his pocket and put it in his cassette deck. At least he had talked to her, he thought. It would be easier to talk with her the next time and maybe then he could ask her out. It probably would have been too forward to have asked her so soon anyway.

Starting to feel a little better, he listened to the music absently and allowed himself to drift off again, imagining the next weekend. He sits alone at a table and orders the same things as the band begins to play. In the middle of the song, she sees him there and smiles. After the show, she walks over to his table, sits down and says, "I was hoping you would come."

It was a particularly pleasing dream.

Buying Time

Barbara Fryer
Huntington Beach

I do not keep a journal although I have tried. So I come obliquely to my concerns by writing novels and short stories. If I did not write, I would not know what I was thinking. I would not know who I am.

Writing is my catharsis, my compass, and my crutch. I say crutch because it allows me to redefine reality. My words can reach across the chasm of the grave and make my mother smile. My words can transplant me into other worlds. And I can play all the parts. In just this past year, I have been a sixty-year-old social science teacher on the lam for bombing a local Bennie Burger; a twenty-two-year-old firefighter now deathly afraid of fire; and an animal liberationist ferrying two stolen chimps across the country.

So I write not to save the world even though I would love to do that, but more selfishly to save and serve myself. Writing, like surfing, positions me in the curve of the movement where nothing else matters but the ride. The turn of shoulder and hip and phrase; the backdrop of the white stuff crashing behind me and the undercurrent of meaning all around me: the rhythm, the pacing, the exhilaration.

As far as my inspiration for this short story, it rose from my obsessiveness with time. The passing of time. Its use and its abuse. To me, time is one of life's true worthy adversaries. And as a Huntington Beach surfer, a walker of the strand, a dog owner, I am forever depositing quarters into that city's parking meters. Each time I do so, I am struck, as my protagonist is, that minutes can be purchased. And it continually delights me and provokes all kinds of fantasies. "Buying Time" was such a fantasy.

Barbara Fryer

Buying Time

Almost an hour ago when Shannon Teele dropped her quarters into the meter and set up her beach chair in the purchased space, she had had her choice of at least a half dozen parking spots on Main Street. Even now, with nine minutes still left, the space to the left was vacant. And from where she sat, she could see the top of a multi-story parking facility a block away. So she really didn't understand why the hairy Iranian with the black socks and tennis shoes kept glaring at her from the front door of his Huntington Beach surfing shop.

Let him stare, she thought, looking away from him just in time to see the computerized meter eat another minute. An eight now registered. Strange how, when you watched time, it sat still like a student locked into submission by the eye of the teacher. But the minute you looked elsewhere, it moved its sneaking fist forward.

She was determined to stare down every minute, especially now, but from the corner of her eye, she saw that Black Socks had moved to the front of his store where he tapped his right foot steady as a pulse. A swirl of beachgoers parted to pass him and then reassembled immediately without a gap in their conversation.

"Lady," he yelled, "that space for customers."

A flock of squawking seagulls passed high over his store, and they gave her an idea. She would try the same tactic she used on the beach when she didn't want to scare the birds. She emptied herself, willing away any sign of a threat. Black Socks would see that she meant him no harm. He would go back into his store and leave her alone. She took three deep breaths, and put her head back, letting the healing balm of the sun melt the uncertainty and anger that had brought her here to Main Street.

But Black Socks flew off nonetheless. "How come you do that here? How come when beach is close? Makes no sense. No sense," he said.

Maybe it didn't make sense, but she didn't care because most of the really important things in life would have never happened if people relied only on logic. Logically, she should have taken the higher paying job in Los Angeles when she first came to California, but she opted for the one in Irvine because she had fallen in love with this corner of Huntington Beach. Within a three-mile radius, she could be in a Texas oil field; a downtown Oklahoma street; horse country; yuppieland or a funky beach city.

And whoever heard of being seduced by a herd of dolphins? Did that make sense? Shannon remembered the October afternoon that Luke had walked out to the Pacific Ocean with his surfboard under his arm and stood over her beach chair, the same one she was sitting in now.

Shannon hadn't known any surfers nor had she had interest in meeting any. As she saw it, the shiny black-suited creatures belonged to the sea where they lorded over towering mountains of water. Out there, they made wild bird noises that sent chills through her. On land, these same sea creatures transformed into ordinary boys and men with zits on their faces and feet that turned outward. And their voice songs grew flat.

A drop had splattered on her book as he danced from foot to foot.

"Did you see that?" he asked.

Her hand tried to absorb the water. "Would you please watch it!" she said.

He stopped so that his drippings fell into the sand. Close up, she saw that he was a little older than she originally thought. Maybe her age. Twenty-three. And he had no zits. His lashes were wet and stuck together; his dark watery eyes were wide and imploring. "You had to have seen it!"

"Seen what?"

"That last wave," he said.

"I don't know who you think you are, but I got more important things to do than watch you surf," she told him.

"Luke...Luke Burrgett," he said like that explained everything. "And it wasn't me I was talking about. It was the dolphins. They took off with me. They were right beside me. I could see them, cutting the wave with me. I swear they were laughing. They were loving it."

A thick strand of dark hair slipped from the rubber band holding his pony tail, and nuzzled his chin. He reached for it and sucked on it as he turned and looked, pensively, out to sea, disappointment etched at the corners of his chapped lips. She was touched by his grace and his sadness at her having missed it.

Shannon knew she should start gathering her things, because the hour she had scheduled for her beach outing was nearly up, but it seemed heartless. It would have been like walking by a beached seal and not making an effort to push him back into the water. She dug her painted toenails into the damp sand. She would wait until he gathered himself. A lone gull flew overhead. She looked up and when she looked back, Luke Burrgett was on his feet.

"Look. There they are now...at two o'clock," he said.

She followed his pointed finger and saw them--six young dolphins riding a four footer. She gasped and hurried to the edge of the water for a better view. The dolphins ripped through the core of water, speeding toward her. They kept coming and coming. Her heart lurched. "They're gonna get beached," she shouted.

The dolphins couldn't have heard her, but at that instant, they flipped in unison and headed out to sea.

She turned toward him and smiled. Then, she had gone back to her chair and talked to him until the winds came up, and the sun began its slow descent.

They had shared so much over the past eighteen months: walks on the beach; coffee on the pier; champagne when she was promoted at work; a camping trip to Big Sur where Luke had decided to go back to college to get his degree; and, of course, the new apartment just two and half blocks from the beach.

But could she share this with Luke? Her mother hadn't been able to share it with Shannon's dad. She hadn't been able to share it with Shannon either. Maybe, if she had, Shannon would know what to expect.

Six more minutes remained on the parking meter. Obviously, her seagull theory wasn't working. Maybe if she tried to explain what she was doing Black Socks would understand. She motioned him closer.

"I know it's kind of silly," she began. "I mean I'm not really buying time, but I am. Where else can you go and do that? It tickles me. That it's available, I mean. That I can come here anytime and buy how ever many minutes I might need it. Do you see?"

"I see you come back."

"I didn't say I would."

"You would." He pointed to the beach a half block away. "That for sunning."

She had come here to figure things out. She hadn't come here to argue. If she had, she could have told him that in the past, she had bought sun screen, flip-flops and even a Pirate Surf Jacket in his shop so, technically, that made her a customer.

Her hand fumbled in her purse. She withdrew a dollar. "Look, if it'll make you feel any better, you can bring me some lip gloss. Okay?"

"Not okay. No curb service. I am businessman." A few people had gathered. He turned to them for support. "Customers come inside store. Right? I do not come outside."

A blond kid in baggy pants with a skateboard under his arm put out his hand. "Give me the dollar. I'll go in the store for you."

"No skateboard inside store," Black Socks said like she would be dumb enough to give this kid her money. He glanced to his doorway. When he saw several of his young clerks hovering there, he waved his hands and shouted, "Inside, Inside."

Shannon returned the dollar bill to her purse. "Have it your way," she said.

"My way, you be gone." He brushed past her, looking up and down the street. "I find police. They make you go."

Her mother's voice rose from the dead. "Shannon, don't make a scene." Scenes involving family members were the great horrors of her mother's life. Only once could Shannon remember her mother inadvertently causing a scene. That was when she grabbed the back of Shannon's dad's pants when he tried to get out of the car to argue with a guy who was battering the hood of their Ford. By the time her dad pulled free and confronted the guy, his pants were down around his ankles, thanks to her mother.

Yes, her mother hated scenes until the very end. When the breast cancer had spread and her doctors gave her three months to live, she had taken to the couch, resigned to the inevitable. Cassie had tried to talk to her, but all her mother could do was cry. Her mother had died two days short of the third month.

Her mother would have picked up the beach chair now and taken it elsewhere. No. Her mother wouldn't have brought the beach chair there in the first place.

The thought jolted Shannon. She grinned for the first time that day. If her mother and she could be so different in one way, then they could be different in other ways.

Black Socks had navigated into the parking spot a young male parking meter attendant, who could have easily passed for an Eagle Scout. "See," he said to the meterman. "Big joke for her."

Shannon had five minutes left on her meter.

"Ma'am, you can't park your beach chair here," the young man said with the full force of the law behind him.

"Show me the code that says I can't," Shannon said.

The sun caught in his silver mouth wires as the kid played with a citation book. "We just enforce the law. We don't carry the lawbooks with us," he said. "Only cars can park here."

"So ticket him." She pointed to the Harley on the right. "He didn't put a cent into his meter. Me...I paid for this time and I'm not giving it away."

"Ticket her," Black Socks coached.

"For what?" she asked.

The kid bites his lip, considering. Finally after several seconds, he told her she could make it easy on herself by folding the chair and leaving. "Or I can call an officer. Which will it be?"

"I'm not going anywhere." She looked at the meter. "At least not for four more minutes."

"I want her out of here. Arrest her," Black Socks said. "Criminals get rights. What about my rights?"

"Sir, why don't you go inside?" the young man said.

"I am naturalized citizen. I have right to stand in front of store. This is land of free."

"And the home of the brave," Shannon added.

A red three flashed inside the meter's glass bubble. The parking attendant sighed. "I need to call the station."

"Then you arrest her?" Black Socks inquired.

"I don't have the authority," the kid said.

"She has more authority than police?"

"I'm not a sworn officer. I don't carry a gun."

A precious sixty seconds dwindled away as the kid tried to explain the difference between a parking meter attendant and a police officer.

"Okay. Okay," Black Socks relented. "Phone behind counter. I watch her."

A trickle of sweat meandered down Shannon's back. In her hurry to shed her clothes, she had put on a black tee shirt. She knew better. She stood and lifted the shirt so air could filter up and cool her. As she did, a piece of paper slipped from her purse pouch. The nurse in Dr. Fowler's office had written the time and day of her biopsy on a card like it was something that Shannon could forget. A tiny ocean breeze caught the hours-old card. It fluttered toward the meter, which had one remaining minute.

Black Socks edged toward her, obviously thinking she was about to make her getaway.

"I'm not going anywhere," she said, energy fusing through her veins. She put another quarter in the meter and purchased ten more minutes. "I figure it should take that long for the cops to get here," she told Black Socks.

"You crazy, lady," he said.

A second later, Shannon saw the black and white car turn off Walnut Avenue onto Main Street. So did Black Socks, who ran to the curb in anticipation.

She sat back down on her beach chair. The warmth from the

asphalt heated her buttocks and thighs. She wouldn't give in without a good fight, she knew that now. And she'd make a scene if she had to. She wouldn't let them cart her off without fighting back. And if they did, she'd insist on her phone call. Her first call wouldn't be to a lawyer; it would be to Luke, asking for help.

Leave Only Footprints

Thanks Jim Coffin Dec. 11 '94

Jim Coffin
Anaheim Hills

Given an opportunity for an early retirement, which I seized with almost embarrassing quickness, has allowed me to commence another career that had been struggling to come to the fore - free lance writing. Attending writers' workshops, purchasing "self-help" manuals and being told in ostinato phrases to "just do it," finally convinced me to "get to it" and the Orange County Short Story Contest was an excellent motivator. In my previous life I was a high school band director, a professor of jazz and percussion at the University of Northern Iowa, a percussion marketing manager working with top drum artists, and I performed in symphony orchestras, jazz bands, as well as having the distinction of being the only gentile in a Jewish cowboy band. But as Dr. Watson stated so often, that story is best left for another time. My main goal is not the great American novel but crafting ingenious and very puzzling mysteries.

Our home overlooks the Anaheim Oak Canyon Nature Preserve, a very special place and an oasis which aided me to shed many years of mind numbing stress. My wife, Kathleen, who, happily, is very much alive, has shared many of my walks and agreed with me that the nature preserve would be an ideal setting for a story. Along with acknowledging her support, I wish to dedicate "Leave Only Footprints" to my new friends, the Oak Canyon naturalistists, who are never too busy to answer questions and whose work with the children is a joy to observe. I urge all to visit and support the center; your footprints will be welcomed!

Jim Coffin

Leave Only Footprints

The little lizard doing push ups on one of the posts caught the elderly man's eye. The sunlight that streamed through the branches of the California oaks engulfed him in warmth as he sat on one of his favorite benches along the Heritage Trail in the Anaheim Oak Canyon Nature Preserve. Dressed in a gray jogging outfit and gray walking shoes, he was slightly overweight, gray haired, in his late sixties, with glasses perched on a slightly bent nose, a mouth etched by a gray goatee. He would have disappeared in a sea of gray if the canyon had been filled with fog as often happens in the spring. But today there was sun and running fingers through his thinning hair, he noted that soon it would be time to wear a cap so as not to get a sunburn on his enlarging bald spot.

"Don't need that to go along with all my other afflictions," he muttered, remembering an old joke about Dave, one of his long departed musician friends.

The gecko, obviously an older one because his back had that black leathery wrinkled look, was still doing his springtime mating moves while looking around hoping that his exertions would be noticed. The man watched for a few moments and then said in that voice we all use when talking to ourselves while driving a car, "Getting in shape for the spring ritual, huh, guy? Did your wife mention that you'd gotten a little bigger around the waist over the winter? In my younger days springtime got me exercising, but it didn't help much."

As if he had heard the man, the gecko stopped, then scurried down the post and disappeared amongst the roots of a large prickly pear cactus whose rose tinged yellow blossoms were just beginning to open. A little breeze stirred the branches of one of the trees and the man said, sotto voce. "I know . . I know Martha. I was moving my lips and talking out loud, but why do you always have to preface a reprimand by calling me an old fool? When I talk to you it just feels better out loud rather than just in my head, and, well, it's more like you're here sitting beside me. But if I hear someone coming, I'll stop so they won't think there's something wrong with me. OK? Satisfied?" The branch seemed to move in an up and down acquiescent manner so he went on.

"Good. That's settled. I'm in kind of a philosophical mood today and you know that sign as you come into Oak Canyon, the one that states, 'You Are Responsible for Knowing the Park Rules.' As I read it this morning, I couldn't help but think that if early in life people had to pass a test before they could enter society on 'You Are Responsible for

Knowing Civilization's Rules,' maybe . . . just maybe," he paused, turned his head, curled his bottom lip over his top, nodded a couple of times, then continued. "You know," scratching the back of his ear, "I just might have something. Let me dig out my notebook and if I can find a pencil in this backpack I'll jot that thought down. Got so much stuff in here, just like your purse used to be, let's see.. good, here's a pencil."

He turned over a few pages in a small green covered spiral notebook, wrote a few hurried lines, stopped writing and then added something else as another thought apparently surfaced. Sticking the notebook and pencil back into the bag, he looked around at the various plants and trees: the cactus garden, sycamores with their star shaped leaves and the California black walnut. The king, though, was the coastal live oak, very common in the Santa Ana mountains and some of them in the canyon were centuries old with gnarled distorted limbs going in all directions, some to the sky, but most angling out, staying close to the ground and providing a green leafy umbrella. A squirrel darted across the asphalt path and into some sumac while a California scrub jay chattered staccato angry phrases at someone or something that had disturbed him.

"I really miss you, my dear," sadly shaking his head. "It's been six months, no wait seven . . . that's right, seven months since you left and I still find it hard to talk to you in our house. Things get in the way there, but here, in the nature center, it seems to be easier."

The man stopped his solo conversation and watched some house finches, their yellow or reddish throats moving as they sang to one another while perched on the edge of an old wagon that was slowly rotting away beside the trail, ivy climbing over the sides and wheels.

"And it is lonely," he commenced again under his breath. "During your last days and for awhile after the funeral, people dropped by or phoned, but then they drifted away, just like we used to do. After I retired we talked about that, about the old W.S.I.T., 'We'll stay in touch,' declaration. People don't, life passes and you have to move on. But I stay busy with my reading and my Sherlock Holmes activities. The Cormorants still meet about once a month and our discussions add a little sanity to what seems to be a daily dose of madness in the papers and on TV. Hmm, the sun really feels good, so I'm going to walk the first part of Roadrunner Ridge up to Quail Trail, and if I'm doing okay maybe continue on to the end. My legs tend to get a little tired, and it seems that someone is always adding more steps as you start the climb."

After adjusting his pack, he started out, noticing that some cactus shoots were beginning to push up through cracks in the surface, stopped to read again one of the plaques telling about the quail, finally reaching the steps leading up to the trail that meanders along the northern edge of the canyon. As he climbed up the wooden bordered dirt steps, the magnificent oaks gave way to the coastal sage scrub, the canyon falling off to his right, while on the left wild flowers, blue mixed with purple, white and yellow hues, fought their way through crevices in the ivy covered rock slabbed hills, and, all thorny below like a certain monarchy, a random thistle wearing a royal purple crown. The sun was moving higher and getting hot. He stopped to remove his jacket and stuff it in the bag, uncovering his Arthur Conan Doyle white tee shirt printed with the famous caricature of the author holding a large magnifying glass. It obviously had been worn a lot because there were a few stains that washing couldn't remove and some of the black ink had faded or disappeared all together. Lizards, young and old, scurried across the path as he wended his way, head somewhat down so he could avoid black ironclad beetles and also not step in a hole or on fallen rocks, which could cause him to twist an ankle and lose his balance. He'd had visions of falling down the hillside into the scraggly sage branches, tearing clothes, breaking bones, and probably ending up shaking hands with a rattlesnake. There were warnings about rattlers. He'd never seen one on the trails, but sure had heard plenty, that buzzing sound telling people to be careful because they were trespassing on Diamondback turf.

The trail continued to wind around, up and down, a freshening breeze stirring the grasses and the flowers while birds sang away in the sage. Glancing up, he watched a Cooper's Hawk soaring on the thermals, ascending ever higher like a biplane in an old black and white movie pirouetting into the clouds.

Reaching the only bench on Roadrunner Ridge, he took off his pack, placed it on the ground and turning caught a rare sight of a mallard and his mate flying just above the trees. About a week before, he had noticed a pair of ducks swimming in the stream, the green head of the mallard constantly bobbing up and down in the water, always moving, while the brown female remained quite still and stoic, her eyes never leaving his face. He'd asked one of the center's naturalists about the ducks and learned that occasionally they would nest along the stream, their natural habitat being the reservoir above the canyon, but the ducklings rarely survived due to predators. Watching their flight, he wondered if they were the same pair and, at the speed they were flying, how in the world they could land in the stream. He chuckled while saying, "Good luck, you two, landing at the Orange County Airport is a piece of cake compared to your flight plan."

After sitting down, he reached into the pack and pulled out a book, opening the pages at the bookmark, adjusted his glasses so the tri-focals would work and began to read. After a few pages, his head began to nod, slipping into a daydream type of slumber that is usually brought on by the combination of a book and sun. Images of days gone by appeared on his mind screen, of the Juanenos and Gabrielinos, nomadic Indian tribes who hunted the animals that came to the stream, now flowing within man-placed boulders and bridges keeping feet dry where before, nature determined the crossing. Sleep was taking greater hold when voices coming from the trail interrupted his reverie. Rousing quickly, though somewhat confused coming out of his brief nap, he stood up just as two matronly ladies, complete with hats, heavy hiking shoes, books and binoculars, came around the bend chatting about the birds they had seen.

"Good morning," they chorused. "Lovely morning, isn't it?"

He agreed as they moved into single file to go around him, not missing a beat in their ornithological discussion after surmising with a glance that he wasn't a member of "The" society. They were correct as he had not gotten into the serious aspect of bird watching, but really enjoyed them as they used the railing on his deck, which overlooked Oak Canyon, for a landing strip.

"Whew," he exclaimed, somewhat sheepishly, "that could have been embarrassing if those two had found me asleep and thought there was something wrong. They looked a bit formidable. Guess I'll have to leave the books at home or read down by the stream out of the sun."

Stuffing the book back in the pack, the man draped it over one shoulder and continued until he was below the cliffs where wind and erosion had eaten away at the surface, leaving cave-like holes. They weren't very deep, yet smaller animals could crawl inside to get out of the rain or maybe sleep. Rounding one of the curves he scared up some quail, their wings flapping furiously as they rose out of the sage by his head, flying across the trail and landing further down the hillside, quickly taking cover in the chaparral. Of all the birds, he liked the quail best. The female, grayish brown with streaks of white and her short little topknot; the plump male with his black head and face outlined in a white beard, a chest covered with yellow and gray speckled feathers that surrounded a rust colored spot on his lower belly, and drooping over one eye, his grenadier, busby-styled plume. But especially, he liked their call, the three syllabled *qua-quer'go, qua-quer' go* which, if they added a note a third higher between quer' and go, would be close to sounding like

Woody Woodpecker's call.

At the junction of Roadrunner Ridge and Quail Trail, which leads down the hill and meets the stream, he saw, lying on top of the Quail Trail sign, a large gecko with faint alligator markings on its back. With head slightly turned up, chest out, eyelids at half-mast, it exuded an air of possession as if to say, "I'm taking over this sign. There are more of us than those birds that have signs; so why don't we have one? Like, Beware - Gecko Crossing."

They continued to look at one another, the lizard statuelike and unafraid, until the man finally decided to head down the hill rather than continuing on the ridge trail, slowly descending and halfway down, looked back over his shoulder up to the sign. Captain Gecko was still in command.

Getting closer to the stream, the sound of rushing water could be heard tumbling over one of many small waterfalls during its serpentine path through and out of the park. Turning right, back toward the Interpretive Center where the naturalists had their office along with an educational museum, he came to a bridge that led to the beginning of Bluebird Loop. This was another favorite trail of his that ran to the eastern edge of the nature center. With oak covered shade it ended up in a prairie grassed path leading to broken down fencing that one could crawl through. The path on the other side of the fence led to a metal gate where you stepped around the post and were back on the main road that went through the center of Oak Canyon. After a moment's hesitation, he continued along the stream deciding to do all of the Bluebird Trail another day.

"Not in the mood," he thought. "Rather spend a little time sitting by the stream; maybe the ducks'll be there, and then end up on that bench under the big oak on Tranquility Trail before I head for home. Anyway, a school class should be arriving soon and it's always a joy to hear their eager inquisitive voices and laughter. Martha really enjoyed the kids."

Walking along the stream, watching the green and sometimes red grasses struggling against the current like streamers outside a store during a Santa Ana blow, his feet crunching on the slippery fallen oak leaves, he felt completely removed from the outside world. Then his eye caught sight of man's intrusion, a styrofoam cup caught on some dead branches lying in brackish back water; later a plastic soft drink bottle, a beer can, all jarring his sensibilities just like the electric poles and wires that stretched along the main road. Coming to the bridge that was just before the slightly listing-to-the-left bench that was his next sit-down, he glanced back up the stream where the water's flow was slower, the banks wider and there were the ducks.

"That landing must have been something," shaking his head. "Probably a quick bank around the trees, flaps down, extend the webbed landing gear, hit the water, put on the brakes, and with much satisfied quacking, wiggle the tail feathers and begin paddling around as if to say 'Nothing to it!' Bravo," softly clapping in appreciation.

He continued to watch them for awhile, leaning on the bridge's redwood stained railing and adding more lines to an already overworked, laugh-creased face. Continuing over the bridge, he changed his mind and went on, crossing over the main road, up the Tranquility Trail steps, taking the left path and finally arriving at his destination. The huge oak had four trunks that over the years had grated together providing a canopy over both bench and trail, with two of the trunks reaching for the sun while other branches twisted and snaked closer to the ground. He dropped the pack on the bench, sat down, leaned back and closing his eyes listened to the non-nature sounds that penetrated even this protected area. Then, for just an infinitesimal moment, it was quiet. No birds sang, no human sounds, no cars or trucks climbing up to where they were working on the water system, nothing. His eyes snapped open at the absence of sound and was suddenly transported back in time, to the hospital where Martha's body and will was slowly being taken over by the disease that marched on to its final knell seven months ago. The picture was still very vivid.

"Have you ever noticed how loud a hospital really is?" remembering. "You'd think that everyone and everything should exist in a hushed respectful atmosphere, not wanting to cause a disturbance. But that isn't so! It's noisy; with intercoms, TVs, consultations, doors banging, people running, phones ringing, food and babies being delivered, machines dispensing, bells dinging, a constant cacophony. Unbelievable!"

It had been like that as he, standing on one side of Martha's bed, had just exchanged glances with Doc Franklin who, standing on the other side and with a very slight sideways head motion delivered that heart wrenching, yet expected, non-vocalized sentence, "Nothing more can be done!" Then a pause, as if everyone was waiting for a reprieve announcement, no sound, and at that very instant, taking both of our hands in hers and giving us that wonderful shy smile, Martha said in a quiet but firm voice, "I want to leave from my home."

She knew without words that the end was approaching and wanted to spend her remaining time amongst her mementos, her books, her music, and the living not the dying. There were no arguments, and the move was made without fuss or fanfare.

He thought about those days and how they would come to Oak Canyon, sit on the various benches and talk about things, both past and current, or just listen to nature's sounds, sometimes just looking at one another. Finally, when she could no longer walk any long distances he would push her in a wheelchair along the main road up by the stream, or they would stop and watch the nature programs and the children. She was in terrible pain most of the time but maintained her cheerful disposition until the day he realized that she had quit fighting. She took to her bed and began to quickly fail.

"Martha, oh, Martha," he said softly. "I was so angry. How could you quit? How could you stop fighting? You couldn't leave me, it wasn't fair, you were always the strong one, and now I'd be alone. Those last days were so hard when you slipped in and out of a coma, sitting by your bed, tears streaming down my face, gripping your hand 'till I thought I might crush your fingers, hanging on, not wanting you to go."

He leaned forward, his elbows on his knees, left hand on top of his right holding up his chin. After a bit, he placed his hands in a praying position, placed them against his lips, finally folding them in his lap and leaned back as tears began to course down his cheeks. Wiping his eyes with his fists he continued softly.

"Oh, how I loved you. How I still love you! Even in my anger, our love took over telling me how selfish I was to want you to continue suffering. That last night I fell asleep in the chair by your bed, and in the morning you were gone. I yelled out loud, 'Why couldn't you have waited until I was awake.' Then I realized, even in death, you were kind and thoughtful and loving. Martha. I miss you so much, so very much, my heart aches just saying those words. Our love was so good and now the house is so lonely and empty without you, but here where we spent so many happy hours I feel very close to you. But it still hurts and I'm lost without you. I still love you so very much."

The leaves whispered, "I know, dead . . . I know."

Leaning forward away from the tree, he took out a checkered handkerchief, blotted his tears and blew his nose. He looked at his watch, slowly got up, picked up the backpack and adjusted the straps, then turned and headed down the trail toward the Interpretive Center. In the middle of the bridge he first heard, then noticed a lot of activity by the feeders along side the building and smiled thinking, "Must be the early-for-lunch-bunch. Maybe if I stopped and watched them awhile it would cheer me up."

He followed the path by the railing, ducked under some tree branches and stopped to take a drink from the fountain by the main trail. Pausing by the entrance to the center, he shook his head, no, and began walking toward the main gate and the street leading to the parking lot. Before reaching the curve in the path, a mother and a child appeared, walking fast as if looking at nature was limited to a schedule rather than leisurely enjoyed. He smiled at them, but they both dropped their heads, the mother grabbing the boy's hand as if afraid and the child following the now very important dictum of never trusting strangers.

"How sad," he reflected, "that in this place, this sanctuary, where all should feel safe, there isn't a closet at the entrance where people could hang up their fears before entering."

Then he heard the mother call out and noticed that lagging behind scuffing the dirt was a little girl, under five years old, dressed in a jeans outfit with her pony tail sticking out the back of a red cap, gazing around in wonderment and not in any hurry. She looked at him with very large, dark trusting eyes and then across her face, which was just beginning to show her life's story, broke a smile, a radiant smile that grabbed the hands of his heart. Then she heard her mother and brother yelling and half-skipping, half-running, kicking up puffballs of dust and with a little wave, disappeared down the path. He watched her go and suddenly felt himself standing a little taller, sadness being replaced with joy and hope as he walked briskly toward the gate. With misted eyes and hanging onto that treasured smile, he slowed his pace by the yellow bordered brown sign to read the last park rule, civilization's eleventh commandment, and his life's epitaph,

"Take only memories, leave only footprints."